DUSK

by
Amy Durham

Other Books by Amy Durham

Once Again (Sky Cove Series #1)
Once And For All (Sky Cove Series #2)

Dedication

In honor and memory of my grandfather,
Adrian Pierson, one of the greatest men I've
ever known. He'd have gotten such a kick out
of his granddaughter being a published author.
If the Adrian in this book seems too good to be
true, it's because the Adrian in my life was truly
that good.

Acknowledgements

I'm always extremely grateful for the wonderful group of writers I'm privileged to be a part of. The authors of the Kentucky Independent Writers group provide tremendous encouragement, inspiration, and camaraderie that I never take for granted. Teresa Reasor and Dawn Laurent-Bourgeious, I cannot thank you enough for the time you invested to read and edit this book. Your input was invaluable and helped me make this story even better. To the ladies of my street team – JeNie, Deanna, Amy, Dawn, Stephanie, Judy, Deana, Anna, and Laura – thank you for believing in me enough that you're willing to tell others about my books. As always, I must thank my husband and my boys for being a constant source of love and entertainment, and for bearing with me as I huddled in my office for days finishing this book. To my dad for his careful editing, and my mom for being my biggest fan, I say a deep thank you. And to you, my readers, thank you for being a part of my dream come true.

CHAPTER 1

The buzz of cheap vodka sang through my body, numbing my stupid reality into complete nothingness. Break-neck speed and three liquored up teenagers probably wasn't the best combination, but none of us cared.

The crowded, city lights of Lexington flickered in the distance behind us, and the sparse lights of Rison, the sleepy Kentucky town where I'd lived my whole life, got closer as Nikki pushed the car way past the speed limit.

"Zoe, don't puke in my car again." Nikki laughed in that slurred, drunken-stupor sort of way, as she turned from the steering wheel to point at me. "If you do you're cleaning it up this time."

Yes, I'd proven myself unable to hold my liquor the last time the three of us had done this. Such a proud moment, for sure. In the front passenger seat, Courtney laughed so hard I thought she'd be the one to hurl.

God, this numbness was bliss. The burn of the alcohol seared away all the crappy parts of my life. Family drama, guilt, uncertainty – all of it – gone. At least that's what I wanted to believe.

It was just after midnight, and the humidity of early August was no better even in the dark. With the windows down, wind rushed around me as I leaned against the backseat, carrying with it the grassy smell of the country. Watching the vast lengths of horse-farm pasture whiz past, I should've been scared, since the roller-coaster speeds couldn't possibly be safe, but being drunk sort of drowns out rationalities such as fear and precautions.

We hadn't seen a car for several miles.

Until the cop car popped into view on the hill in front of us, and Nikki had to jerk the wheel and swerve out of his lane to avoid hitting him. As the cruiser passed us, Courtney and I turned to look out the back window just in time to see the blue lights come on.

"Shit!" Nikki said. "Hang on!"

My shoulder slammed hard into the back door as Nikki made a split-second right turn onto a side road. Barreling down the winding lane, houses and barns sporadically appeared and disappeared as she sped on. I craned my neck around and saw the police lights nearing the turnoff we'd taken, and without slowing, Nikki switched off her lights, plunging us into blackness. This far from the city, the sky sparkled with bright stars. It would've been pretty... under normal circumstances.

Nikki made the next two curves without trouble, but a hairpin left turn was not so kind. She slammed the brakes and the car fishtailed, throwing me all over the backseat, my other shoulder colliding with the driver-side door. It hurt like a bitch, but I was too busy fighting to keep the ocean of liquor in my stomach from swimming upstream to pay much attention to the pain.

But before I had the chance to grace Nikki's backseat with the contents of my stomach, the fishtailing ended as we plowed into something – a tree, a ditch, a utility pole – and this time my head smashed against the door. Digging my fingers into the leather upholstery, I tried without success to steady myself.

The crunch of crashing metal was deafening as pain exploded in my head, fireworks went off behind my eyelids, and I slid to the floorboard.

Police sirens sounded in the distance, coming closer. I knew that the approaching cop was not a good thing, but the haze in my head refused to let me remember why. Blinking, I tried to get clear of the mental fog and sit up, but instead just collapsed on the floorboard of the car again. Nikki and Courtney moaned in the front seat, and Nikki fumbled uselessly with the driver's door. Something inside me said I should get out and run, but why?

The sirens grew louder and louder until I was sure the police car had to be right beside us. Out of nowhere, arms came around me. Strong arms. Warm arms. Curling against him, I gave myself over to the safety and security that enveloped me, close and tender, like an old blanket.

And then it was as if I was floating, flying even. Was I dreaming? Had I left my body? I didn't know, and I didn't care. The breeze kissed my skin with a velvety touch, and the strength of his body radiated into mine. Sleep eased toward me, and I welcomed it with the assurance that I was safe and protected.

CHAPTER 2

A sledgehammer pounded away at my head and my tongue seemed hot-glued to the roof of my mouth. When I shifted positions, the rustle of sheets and the cushy pillow beneath my head told me I was in my bed. But even the soft sheets and pillow couldn't dim the general, achy crud I felt all over my body. Geez, even my pinkies hurt.

I could tell without looking that I was still in my shorts and tank top. I'd slept in my clothes. Fantastic. I must've been completely wasted when I got home. I started to shake my head in disgust of my own behavior, but thought better of it when the sledgehammer started up again.

The slight movement made my stomach swim, and the entire night came rushing back. Bored, alone, and depressed at home. The phone call from Nikki and Courtney. The liquor none of us were old enough to drink.

God, the liquor. I'd lived seventeen years without getting smashed, but this summer I'd fixed that. After last night I could go the rest of my life without experiencing it again.

With startling clarity I recalled the police car and Nikki's furious attempt to out run him. She'd crashed her car. I remembered that part as the side of my head screamed in pain. Surely he'd caught up to us after that, but I had no memory of it.

How did I get home? How did I end up in my bed?

Oh lord, had the cop called my mom? Or worse yet, driven me home in the police car? This was going to suck royally. Mom was already pissed at me for my previous transgressions, all of which involved Nikki, Courtney, and alcohol. Now she'd be totally livid. I might never get my car keys back.

I tried opening my eyes. It was possible my brain would explode once my lids lifted, but maybe that wasn't such a bad thing. At least my head wouldn't hurt anymore.

A gray haze filled my vision, and I was quite sure it was a result of the hangover and not actual fog in my bedroom. The tiny slits in my eyelids let in faint illumination, like those dim-lighted moments before the sun actually came out. Gradually, my room came into focus... the iPod dock on my dresser, the pile of laundry in the floor, the cute, dark-haired boy on my lavender beanbag.

Cute boy? Good grief, I must still be drunk if I was hallucinating a hottie.

I blinked, not without effort and pain, clearing away some of the haze, and sure enough, my beanbag was empty. My heart fell. I was kind of disappointed. If I'd been non-hangover-burdened, I might've stuck my bottom lip out.

Resigned to my aloneness, I closed my eyes and decided more sleep would be a good idea. Maybe the hangover would clear up a bit. I'd need the rest later when I had to face my mom.

I heard my mom come in my room some time afterward. I pretended to still be asleep, hoping she'd go on to work and I could put this confrontation off until later, when hopefully my head wouldn't feel like a giant bowling ball crashing into enormous bowling pins. But, no such luck.

She sat down on the bed, the mattress dipping only slightly under her weight. I felt her brush my hair off my forehead, the gesture protective and maternal. A lump formed in my throat. Why was she being gentle with me after what I pulled last night? However tender she behaved with me, I was quite sure my punishment would be anything but.

"Zoe," she whispered. "We need to talk before I go to work."

I opened my eyes, taking my time just in case the light decided to burn my retinas. Thankfully the headache seemed to have eased enough that I could tolerate the minimal illumination in the room. Looking up at my mom, I had no idea what to say.

"I came in your room last night," she began, keeping her voice soft and low. "Well, technically it was this morning. You were home by one o'clock, already in bed. After they way you snuck out, I was kind of surprised."

Confusion swirled in my brain. Somehow I'd gotten home and in my bed by one in the morning. And Mom didn't sound mad, so I must not have come home in a police car. Which still begged the question – how had I gotten home?

My temples throbbed and I decided I'd worry about how I'd gotten home later. Heavy consideration was sure to bring my headache roaring back full force.

Still, I said nothing to Mom.

"But Zoe, you were practically passed out and you reeked of alcohol." She sounded more disappointed than anything. And that tone of voice was worse than being yelled at.

I unglued my tongue from the roof of my mouth and managed to eek out a ratchety-sounding "Sorry".

"Baby, I know you're hurting, and I know you're just acting out. I know this is all a result of what happened with your father. I want to help you, but I don't know what to do to reach you. I'm at my wits end, Zoe."

If I'd somehow gotten out of that car last night and escaped having to face the cops, I was taking that as the mother of all wake-up calls. No more Nikki and Courtney and alcohol binges.

Good God, had I walked all the way home? Thoughts of what could've happened as I'd meandered home, drunk off my ass, were enough to make my stomach turn even without the hangover.

"Won't happen again," I whispered. Hopefully she knew I meant it, because I didn't have the energy or brain function to explain it further. And there was the fact that I couldn't really tell her about the car wreck and my big epiphany without incriminating myself in the process.

"Well, that's a change of attitude," she said. "You've been completely unapologetic about your behavior all summer."

"I mean it," I said. "No more."

Mom nodded. "I'm giving you the benefit of the doubt."

"Thanks." I managed a half smile.

"Nikki and Courtney were arrested last night. Nikki was driving drunk and crashed her car. She and Courtney weren't seriously hurt, but it could've been much worse. There was marijuana in the car too."

Holy crap. I hadn't smoked any weed, but only because I had no idea they'd had it. If not for the police chase and car wreck, I probably would've lit up before the night was over.

"Nikki's mom called me because she thought you might've been with them," Mom said. "You don't know how relieved I was to find you here."

Yeah, if you only knew.

I closed my eyes. This conversation was not helping my hangover. The mystery of how I'd ended up at home in bed while Nikki and Courtney were getting arrested was enough to create a headache under normal circumstances.

"I've got to go to work, but I've left a glass of water and some ibuprofen on your nightstand. Take a couple and drink the water, when you feel up to it."

I nodded, eyes still shut.

"I'll check back in at lunch." I felt the mattress shift as she stood up. "I believe you about not drinking anymore, but I hope you'll understand that I'm going to have to keep your car keys for a bit longer."

Yeah, I figured that was coming. And honestly, I was going nowhere in the near future anyway. Unless it was to worship the porcelain goddess.

"You should call Vivian," she added just before she left the room. "She's been a good friend to you, and I'm sure she'll understand why you've been so distant this summer."

And didn't that lay the guilt on even thicker?

I listened for her car to crank and pull out of the driveway then forced myself to sit up. I managed to make it without falling over, and even more amazing, I managed to maneuver the childproof lid off the medicine bottle. I downed three ibuprofen and half the glass of water, then burrowed back under the covers.

Glancing at my beanbag, I half hoped to find my dark-headed guy again. Of course, he was not there. Just as well. If I'd been drunk enough to bring home some random guy I'd be in way more trouble than I already was. Dad would've freaked out to find a guy in my bedroom.

And just like that, the ache returned and settled like a ton of concrete on my chest. Dad couldn't freak out anymore, because he was dead. And the truth was, after everything that had happened before he died, I wouldn't have listened to him anyway.

Simultaneous guilt and grief was a nasty combination.

CHAPTER 3

A week later school started. I still had no car keys, so Mom dropped me off. I'd kept my promise and had not touched another drop of alcohol. Of course, it did help that Nikki and Courtney were dealing with their own drama after getting arrested and were probably in no condition to call me up and offer to provide the stuff.

Thanks to some state funding that came our way three years ago, the new Rison High School was a far cry from the Jurassic era school building where I'd spent my freshman year. In small-town Kentucky, it wasn't exactly state-of-the-art, but the place looked tons better than the drab gray of the previous institutional structure, and even now it still had that *new school* smell.

The normal summer catch-up talk filled the building, but I heard nothing about Nikki and Courtney's time in the county lock-up. I figured they wanted to keep that quiet. But in typical high school fashion, there was no shortage of other stuff to gossip about. Apparently, Heather Mossman, a junior, was pregnant. Great. Another statistic. Also according to the talk in the hallways, Tim Fowler and Cody Walsh had gotten into a huge fight at the county fair, which resulted in the police being called and assault charges being filed. Apparently one had keyed the other's truck over a girl.

Even as I shook my head at the absurdity of it all, inside, I cringed at how close I'd come to being part of the rumor mill. In a school this small, there was nothing worse than being the subject of gossip. It didn't even matter if what was being said was true or not, people would blather on and on about stuff, exaggerating as they went, and before long everyone was an expert on your life.

Headed up the hall toward my homeroom, I kept my head down and didn't approach anyone or enter into the conversations. Considering how I'd spent my summer, invisible seemed like a pretty good idea.

Approaching Mrs. Harvey's classroom, I found my best friend, Vivian Rogers, waiting for me. At least I hoped she was still my best friend. Though we'd talked a few times, I'd snubbed her pretty much all summer, in favor of Nikki and Courtney and the rebelliousness I'd found with them. I had no excuse, no real way to explain myself, other than admitting I'd been a stupid fool. I only hoped Viv would be forgiving.

"Hey Viv," I said, hoping the contriteness I felt came through in my voice. "I'm sorry I didn't call much over the summer. I was just –"

"It's okay." Viv just smiled, forgiveness and hurt showing equally in her eyes. Even through the hurt, she still tried to understand. "I know you were just fighting your way back after losing your dad."

"I behaved like a moron."

"Yes, you did," she agreed. "Are you done with those two skanks?"

"Absolutely," I said. "And I really am very sorry. For everything."

"And I accept." She nodded her head toward Mrs. Harvey's room, her curly red hair bouncing around her face. "Let's head to homeroom."

Relief warmed me from the inside. Just like that, things were back to almost normal between Viv and me. Well, sort of. She'd accepted my apology, but I knew I'd still need to prove myself to her. Forgiveness didn't necessarily mean complete trust just yet. But, if Viv could try to get past my stupidity, I had to believe that I could find some part of my old self – my *real* self – too.

Nikki and Courtney made their first appearance at lunch. Well, I figured they'd been at school the whole day, but since I was enrolled in honors classes, and they were... well... *not* enrolled in honors classes, I'd been able to avoid them.

Not so lucky in the cafeteria, which naturally smelled of some bland, generic vegetable steaming away. The two of them stood just inside the door. Though Vivian knew I'd spent some time sowing some wild oats with Nikki and Courtney, she had no idea about the night of the wreck. No one did.

Not even me, if you got right down to it.

"Viv, why don't you get us a table," I said. "I'll be right there."

"You sure?" she asked.

I nodded. I had to get this over with. I figured the two of them didn't want word to spread about their arrests, which meant they couldn't announce my involvement without implicating themselves. But that didn't mean they weren't going to try to make me miserable.

As soon as she stepped away, I turned to face Nikki and Courtney.

"You freaking ran out on us." Courtney's voice dripped with contempt. It was difficult to take her seriously with her low-cut shirt and ill-fitting push-up bra shoving her cleavage out at a very unnatural angle. Not to mention the cut-off shorts that clearly did not meet the school dress code. Also distracting was her artificial black hair, which looked like someone had resurfaced the black top of a driveway with her head. Combine that with the hoop protruding from her eyebrow piercing, and Courtney was a hot mess. It was a shame, really. She'd probably be kind of pretty without all that.

"Left us there to take the blame for everything," Nikki added with a snarl.

Yes, I'd been drunk. Yes, I would've been in big trouble for that. But I hadn't been driving, so technically that offense was Nikki's alone. I decided I probably shouldn't point that out.

Even with the fuchsia streaks in her blond hair, she didn't look trashy like Courtney. I was pretty certain

Courtney's dye job came from a bottle she got at the discount store, while Nikki's came from a pricey salon. And that just highlighted the difference between the two of them. Nikki was the money behind the operation, and Courtney was the tag-along.

"Look, I was just as drunk as you guys," I said, keeping my voice low. "I barely remember the wreck, much less what happened afterward. I don't remember getting out of the car, and I have no idea how I got home. I guess I walked."

"Yeah right." Nikki stepped closer, putting her face inches from mine. "You expect us to believe that you wandered over three miles to your house and have no memory of it? How stupid do you think we are?"

Answering that question honestly would probably get me punched in the face.

Ebony black hair caught my attention from across the cafeteria. It belonged to a really tall guy dressed in faded jeans and a light blue tee shirt, and even though his back was to me, I knew he was new here. Those broad shoulders were far more imposing than any shoulders that usually walked these halls. Though I mentally willed him to turn around so I could see his face, he tossed an empty water bottle in the trash and exited the lunchroom through the doors on the opposite side. On his way out, I caught a glimpse of what looked like black leather biker-style boots.

Interesting. Too bad I hadn't gotten a good look at him.

Oh well. Rison was a small school. I'd see him again eventually.

Nikki's tapping foot brought me back to my unpleasant reality.

"I don't know what else to say." I looked at both of them. "I remember pretty much everything up until the wreck, and then it's just blank. I hit my head when we crashed and after that I don't know what happened."

"You skipped out and left us to get arrested, while you came out squeaky clean." Courtney stepped closer as well. "We're lucky Nikki's dad knew the right people to call, but it's still not over for us."

"I'm sorry, I really am." That much was true. I'd been there in that car with them, and I really was sorry that things had gone so badly. On the other hand, I was not sorry that the wreck had scared the stupid out of me. "But I can't tell you what happened because I don't remember."

"We may not be able to prove you were in that car with us, but don't think you won't pay for abandoning us to take the heat," Nikki said, just before the two of them stalked off.

Fantastic. Nikki and Courtney's revenge radar was so not where I wanted to be.

Viv and I both had Political Science with Mr. Austin last period. I loved Mr. Austin. He was the sponsor of the Student Government Organization, so as president of my class freshman, sophomore, and junior year, I'd gotten to know him pretty well.

Which made his class the toughest one all day. First of all, he patted me on the back and told me he was so sorry to hear about my dad. I managed not to tear up, but it was a close call. Second, he pointed out the poster about Student Government Elections, and told me he was looking forward to working with me again.

I hadn't thought about Student Government all summer. And the idea of putting myself out there, making speeches, being the advocate for the senior class? After the past few months I couldn't imagine a scenario where I'd feel comfortable with all that. But Mr. Austin's enthusiasm kept me from saying so.

I'd figure out a way to tell him I wasn't running for office. Just not today.

Viv saved me when she came in like a whirlwind, grabbing my arm and pulling me toward a row of desks.

"Did you hear about the new guy?" she asked, her eyes wide with animation. Viv always got excited when she was the first to share something.

"No," I said, glad I could answer truthfully. I hadn't *heard about* the new guy, though I was pretty sure I'd *seen* him.

"Moved here from Florida," she said. "At least that's what I heard from Jennifer, and she helps out in the office during fifth period, so I figure she knows. And get this. He rode to school on a motorcycle!"

A motorcycle? Wow. That was a first for Rison High.

"Why didn't we notice that this morning?" I asked.

"He didn't come in to enroll until just before lunch. I heard he's living with his aunt while his parents are off on some top secret job somewhere in Europe."

To be so sensible and down-to-earth, Viv loved gossip more than anyone I knew.

"Did you catch his name?" I was dying to know if tall, dark, and built had a name to match his looks.

"Not yet, but I'm working on it," she said with a wink.

I rolled my eyes and giggled at her, thinking how glad I was to be back in a routine with my best friend. Nikki and Courtney had been poor substitutes for Vivian.

I waited on the front sidewalk with the other kids whose parents picked them up. By and large they were all either too young to drive or unfortunate enough to have overprotective parents who wouldn't let them ride the bus. Then there was me – a licensed driver who'd lost her keys thanks to reckless behavior.

I saw *him* – ebony hair guy from the cafeteria – just as I noticed Mom driving down the street and pulling into line with the other parents. The motorcycle was hard to miss, large and gleaming black, standing between two pick-up trucks looking completely out of place and totally cool at the same time.

He picked up the helmet and turned to look straight at me, like he meant to. Like among all the other people in the parking lot and waiting on the sidewalk, he'd picked me out on purpose.

I couldn't help but look back. There was something so familiar about him. Even from a distance I could tell he was tall, at least a head taller than the boy getting into the truck next to him. His hair, dark and just long enough to turn up on the ends, was just the right amount of messy. I couldn't see the color of his eyes, but the deep dimples in his cheeks flashed when he smiled at me.

He. Smiled. At. Me.

A gentle breeze swirled around me and seemed to warm me from the inside. A sense of *rightness* simmered and hummed around in my soul, as if somehow he'd flipped the switch that had shut off when my dad died.

I smiled back, but only halfway. This moment was so surreal. My mind didn't exactly believe the images my eyes were sending, and my heart was having real trouble with the emotional side of things.

He nodded, acknowledging my smile, and just as I was about to take a huge risk and wave at him, a car horn beeped.

Mom.

When I looked back toward motorcycle dude, his back was to me as he strapped on his helmet. Just as well. I was seconds away from making a total fool of myself.

But his smile and the dimples stayed with me the entire drive home.

We lived on Stableview Road, a little country lane a couple of miles off the main highway that ran through Rison. Though it wasn't the center of the action, it wasn't exactly the boondocks, especially since there were four other houses down our road, along with the lovely, rolling pastures of Bryton Farms, one of many horse farms in our neck of the woods.

"I hope today wasn't too awkward," Mom said, as we neared our driveway.

"Nikki and Courtney had their say at lunch," I replied, conveniently leaving out the part about my being in the car when Nikki crashed. "They don't get why I dropped them."

"Well, you've made the right decision. I hope you still believe that."

I nodded. "Viv and I are fine. For the most part. She was very forgiving."

Mom smiled, pulling up beside the house. "Let's see how the first few weeks of school go, and maybe you can have your car keys back."

That thought perked me up a bit.

Mom went on. "I know you haven't wanted to talk about your dad, but at some point we're going to have to. I'm here when you're ready."

And that thought slammed me back down.

"There's not much to talk about," I said. "We said it all the day he walked out on us."

"He didn't walk out on us, Zoe." She stopped and turned to me, sighing heavily. "There's plenty left to say, and I think you know that. But I won't push you. Yet. I know that what happened is more than you can easily wrap your mind around. But you can't hold it all inside forever."

I said nothing. Just opened my car door and started to get out.

Mom's hand on my arm stopped me.

"I've got to get back to the office. I'll be home at my regular time."

"Okay."

"Think about what I said, Zoe."

I stepped out of the car and shut the door.

She backed out of the drive, and I watched her car disappear as she headed back to town. I dug my keys from my purse, but just as I turned to go inside, the sound of an approaching vehicle caught my attention.

It was louder than most cars that regularly drove this road.

That's because it wasn't a car at all.

It was a motorcycle. A big, black one.

Even with the helmet obscuring his hair, I knew it was the ebony-haired guy from school. The light blue shirt was my first clue. But really, how many black motorcycles ran the roads in Rison? He slowed as he passed my house, looking over with a wave. This close to the road, I could even see his grin and the dimples.

He and his bike were out of sight, further down the road toward Ms. Turner's house, when I realized I hadn't waved back.

CHAPTER 4

The advantage of starting the school year on Thursday was that Friday came quickly, and on the second day of school all buzz centered on the new guy.

The motorcycle seemed to be the biggest topic of conversation. I had to admit it was pretty cool. No one had ever driven a motorcycle to Rison High. I remembered seeing him yesterday, in the school parking lot and then again riding down my road after school. Despite the biker-persona, his eyes had been kind, and I found myself curious to know more about him. Like maybe his name.

Halfway to my locker, I caught sight of him. With Nikki Hughes. And Courtney Powell. Nikki was clearly on the prowl, judging by the way she slid her hand down his arm. Gag me.

Looking the other way, I pushed my way through the crowded hall and reached my locker. Naturally, Nikki's voice rose louder as I got closer.

"There's a party at Chad Blevins's place tonight," she said. "All the important people will be there."

Like Nikki, Chad's parents had money, and didn't mind spending it on their son, to the point that Chad was as spoiled as Nikki, with just as big a sense of entitlement. I was quite sure there would be plenty of alcohol at Chad's get-together, and probably other stuff I didn't want to think about.

How had I ever thought I wanted any part of that craziness? Then I remembered the numbness I'd been looking for. The empty nothingness that had seemed to help me escape the awful mix of emotions I'd had after my father left. Then died.

Thank goodness I'd realized how insane an idea that had been before I screwed up any worse.

"I can swing by and pick you up." Nikki's voice screeched above the noise of slamming lockers and teenage chatter. "Or we could take your bike."

For a split second I considered asking her what was going on with the drunk driving charges, but I really didn't want to stoop to her level.

"No thanks," came an unfamiliar voice. And what a nice voice it was. Deep and rich, and different from any voice I'd ever heard. "But it was nice to meet you."

I hung my backpack in my locker and looked around for Viv, while Nikki continued to call after biker-guy. I rolled my eyes. He'd been polite, but pretty clear. He wasn't interested. Yet she persisted.

Desperation was not an attractive quality in a female.

Looking to my left, I saw Viv making her way down the hall. And then *he* stepped into my vision, blocking out Viv and the rest of the chaos in the hallway.

Umm, wow. He was even better up close. The ability to speak left me.

"Hey," he said, and considering he was standing so close, I knew he was talking to me.

I looked up. Way up. He had to be over six feet tall. And looked straight into the most gorgeous set of baby blues I'd ever seen. The deep green shirt he wore today accentuated the color of his irises.

Black hair and blue eyes were totally hot together.

"I saw you yesterday," he continued, unaffected by my stunned silence. "I'm Adrian."

Adrian. It suited him. His name was just as beautiful he was.

I should talk. Say something. Introduce myself. Wipe the drool from my chin.

"Zoe," I squeaked, cringing at how stupid I sounded. "Zoe Gray."

"Adrian Shaw." He stuck his hand out, waiting for me to shake it.

I stared at his hand. He wanted me to put my hand in his, and even as I told myself it was just a simple greeting, the thought of feeling his skin against mine left me frozen.

Snap out of it! Act like you have a brain, not just raging hormones!

I gripped his hand. His fingers closed around mine, and everything inside me went still, calm... *right*. The noise around me stopped. The bustle of the kids in the hall faded away. And I found myself lost in the feeling of my hand in his, drowning in the way his eyes searched mine.

"I'm living with my aunt, Maggie Turner." His voice snapped me out of my trance, and at the same time anchored me to him even more. "She lives down the road from you, I guess."

"Yes." I nodded, pulling my hand from his with a healthy amount of regret. "I know her. She bakes cakes, right?"

"Right." He leaned a shoulder against the locker next to mine, as if settling in for a long conversation. "I'm sure we'll be seeing each other, since we live so close."

"I guess," I said, turning to look at my locker, in an attempt to *not* stare at him. Besides, I needed to grab my Pre-Calculus book for second period. I didn't want to have to make a trip back to the locker.

"You going to that party she was just talking about?" he asked.

"Um, no." I almost laughed out loud. Where was my Pre-Cal book? I'd taken it home to look through it, as if glancing ahead would somehow magically make me understand it all. I could've sworn I had it in my backpack when I left home this morning.

"Not your speed?"

"Not anymore." I unzipped my backpack further, peering inside. No Pre-Cal book. This was not going to make a good impression on Ms. Faulkner. "I wasn't invited anyway."

"That may have been a compliment," he said. I felt him lean closer, looking over my shoulder. "What are you looking for?"

"My Pre-Cal book. I had it in my backpack when I left home. At least I thought I did."

Just then the warning bell rang, signaling that I had two minutes to get to homeroom. Great. Second day of school and already I was going to show up to Pre-Cal unprepared. As if there wouldn't be enough of that once we got started with homework and I showed up half-finished because I was clueless.

"Maybe it'll turn up." He pushed away from the lockers and looked at me one last time. "Nice meeting you."

Okay, forget Pre-Cal. I needed to be nice to him. I'd kind of like it if he talked to me again. Even though he was one hundred percent out of my league.

"Yeah, if it's not here it's in my room at home," I said. "Nice meeting you too."

He winked and smiled, then turned into the flow of kids heading down the hall. Warm from my toes all the way to my head, I reached in my locker and grabbed what I needed, minus the Pre-Cal book, and headed toward homeroom.

Viv was waiting at the door for me. "We are so talking later."

The signs for student government elections greeted me as I left homeroom. Mr. Austin must've hung them up while we were in class.

"Hey," Viv said, pointing at the sign. She, like probably everyone else in the building, just assumed I'd run for class president again.

I shook my head. "I'm not running."

"Why not?" She grabbed my arm and pulled us both to a stop.

I shrugged. "Too much has happened. I just can't deal with the spotlight."

Viv sighed, then nodded. "I understand. But Mr. Austin's going to be disappointed."

"I'm trying to figure out how to tell him," I replied, as we started walking again.

As we neared the hall with the math classrooms, I remembered my absent Pre-Cal book. Something in me whispered that I should check my locker one more time. A breeze swirled around me, like someone stood behind me fanning with a piece of paper. I slowed, glancing behind me and seeing nothing but kids headed to second period.

Viv slowed as well, and I told her to head on to her second class. We'd catch up with each other at lunch. Before she disappeared into the crowd of people lining the hallway, I saw Brett Martin fall in step beside her. Brett was some kind of baseball virtuoso and one of those rare creatures who was both super popular and genuinely nice. To my knowledge, Brett and Vivian had never interacted, but judging by the smiles and flirty looks going on, they'd managed to get to know one another. I made a mental note to ask her about it later.

The notion of checking my locker again urged me on, as if by some miracle my Pre-Cal book had now materialized, but I could not shake the feeling that I should look once more.

I upped my pace, weaving through the traffic in the hall, so that I could do the locker-check and still get to Mrs. Faulkner's room on time. Naturally, I met Nikki and Courtney on their way to the restroom, and endured Nikki's nasty glance. In addition to being pissed at me for the fact that I mysteriously escaped getting arrested, unlike the two of them, now she was clearly miffed about the fact that Adrian spoke to me. Correction... he blew her off in order to speak to me.

Take that, ho bag.

Remembering his ice blue eyes and his sweet smile, I found it hard to care that Nikki was now doubly gunning for me.

The breeze picked up again, moving against my neck and pushing me the last few steps to my locker. If I didn't know better, I'd swear someone was behind me blowing air on my skin. Weird sensation, but not an unpleasant one.

I made quick work of my combination, preparing myself to find nothing once the door opened.

My Pre-Cal book stared up at me from the bottom of my locker. Not in my backpack, but the bottom of the locker.

Huh?

I rewound my brain to first thing that morning. I'd come up the hall, hearing random people talking about the new biker-guy. Saw him talking to Nikki. Opened my locker. He appeared. We talked. I hung up my backpack. Looked for my Pre-Cal book.

For the life of me, I could not remember removing the book from my backpack or putting it in the bottom of the locker. Of course, I'd been distracted by Adrian's attention… and his seriously gorgeous face… but I doubted that I'd tossed that book to the bottom of the locker.

I never used the bottom of the locker. I always hung my backpack on the hook. Much easier to grab what I needed when it was at eye level.

Yet there was no denying that the Pre-Cal book was there.

I bent to pick it up, and when I stood, Adrian was there.

"Told you it would turn up."

He flashed his dimples in a quick grin, then winked and walked off.

Again.

CHAPTER 5

Turned out having my textbook for Pre-Calculus didn't make much difference. Yes, I was able to write down the page number for my homework assignment. No, I was not able understand how to do it.

Well, I *thought* I understood it. It all made sense when Mrs. Faulkner explained it and showed us examples. At home, sitting at the picnic table in the backyard, trying to do my homework on my own, I was lost.

Unfortunately, I had not inherited the math-genius genes from my dad, the mechanical engineer, and he'd been the one to help me get through two years of Algebra and one year of Geometry. But he wasn't here to help me now.

And truthfully, even if he was here, I probably wouldn't even speak to him, much less accept his help. I think it's an unwritten rule that when you cheat on your wife, you lose homework help privileges with your daughter.

In an attempt to drown out the memories I kept buried, I picked up my phone and clicked to open my email. I'd kept away from most social media since my life blew up, but email seemed safe enough. No enormous list of unread messages waited for me, however at the top of my inbox was a message from Lea Graham.

Lea was kind of my pen pal. Not through any official pen pal organization or anything like that. Her parents worked as missionaries in Kenya, and two years ago, their family visited the church that Mom, Dad, and I attended together. So close in age, the two of us hit it off and exchanged email addresses. We'd been keeping in touch ever since, although her messages were less frequent now that they were back in Kenya, where the internet connection could be sketchy.

I'd heard from her once over the summer, not long after the funeral, and I just couldn't bring myself to respond to her.

Taking a deep breath, I opened the message and began to read.

Hello Zoe. I hope that you are well. Here in Mombasa, the activity center that my parents run has received seven new computers. I'm typing on one of them now! It's very nice for the kids who come here in the afternoons to be able to use technology to learn and play. Most of them have never used a computer. You should see their eyes light up when they sit in front of the screens. Sometimes when I find myself wishing for the conveniences I got used to while we were in the states on furlough, I just look at these kids and remember how very fortunate I am. However, we are expecting a new computer for our home, and I am very excited about that possibility! I do so look forward to your stories of traditional high school and all the fun things going on! I hope to hear from you soon. Much love, Lea.

Without replying I closed the message and set my phone on the table. I felt like crap for feeling sorry for myself even the tiniest bit when the kids she saw every day lived in conditions I couldn't even imagine. I couldn't write to her and pretend everything was fine. Yet how could I tell her the truth? I didn't even know what the truth was anymore.

And the thought of putting it all in words make me sick to my stomach.

I missed my dad, and yet at the same time part of me was still so angry at him. And I had nowhere to direct that anger, thanks to wet roads, bald tires and a hydro-planing pick-up truck.

I shook my head in disgust and looked down at my homework. Compared to my messed up emotional state, being clueless in Pre-Cal seemed like a minor annoyance.

Wrapped up in my own internal drama – and still staring blankly at my textbook – I didn't hear footsteps approaching. But I did notice the black biker boots that appeared next to the picnic table.

Adrian.

"I have Mrs. Faulkner after lunch," he said, throwing one leg over the bench to sit next to me. "Bet we have the same assignment."

"Probably so." I wondered what in the world he was doing, showing up here on a Friday afternoon.

"I finished my homework a few minutes ago. Need some help?"

"Can you read minds?" I was only half joking. Him showing up here just as I was about to throw in the towel on the second day of school was terribly coincidental. But if he was good at math, who was I to argue?

He shrugged. "Math comes easy."

"Where's your bike?" I asked, still kind of stunned that he'd just appeared.

"I walked."

Okay. He wasn't very forthcoming with information, but maybe that's all there was to it. Perhaps he just went out for a walk.

"You didn't seem too enthused about Pre-Cal when we talked this morning, so I had a hunch you might need some assistance with the homework." He scooted closer and picked up my pencil. "And it's in my nature to be helpful."

Over the next hour, I found out that he was telling the truth. Both about math coming easy and about being helpful. And in between working problems, I'd managed to gather a little information about him.

"You moved from Florida, right?" I asked.

"No secrets around here, I guess," he said with a laugh.

"Not so much. Small town and all."

"Yeah, I lived in Florida."

"How'd you get here?" Apparently he wasn't going to volunteer information, but he seemed willing to answer, so I kept asking.

"My parents are in Hungary." He pointed to a sample problem he'd worked on my scrap paper. "Now you try the one in the book."

I started on the problem, but kept up with the questions. "What are they doing in Hungary?"

"My dad teaches English as a second language, so he travels a lot. He's working in Budapest for the next several months."

"You didn't want to go with them?"

"I've been to Europe before," he said, nudging me and pointing toward the problem in the book. "And I wanted to finish high school in the states. So I came to live with Aunt Maggie."

I nodded, figuring his explanation was decent. I got back to work on the problem, and decided to let it go and just get my work done. With his assistance, I not only finished my homework, but also managed to grasp it enough to have at least a basic understanding.

Homework completed, he had no reason to stick around, and I found myself toying with the idea of asking what he was doing this weekend. But that would be really lame, like I was as desperate as Nikki trying to convince him to go to that party. So I said nothing, even though my weekend with no car keys stretched before me like an eternity… two long days of bored-out-of-my-skull.

Well, boredom was better than running with Nikki and Courtney.

Adrian seemed in no hurry to leave even though the homework was done. To avoid an awkward silence, I busied myself with packing the Pre-Cal supplies back into my book bag, while trying to come up with something witty to say.

"So I'm going with my aunt to Lexington tomorrow," Adrian said, breaking the silence and saving me from saying something that would've no doubt sounded dumb. "Helping set up a wedding cake and other stuff for a reception."

Maggie Turner, Adrian's aunt, with whom he was apparently living for the foreseeable future, was a baker-slash-caterer. She was known around Rison as the "Cake Lady", and on the few occasions I'd had to enjoy her baked goods, I'd been impressed. Apparently news of her skills had spread to neighboring Lexington, which was great for her business.

Adrian went on. "But I was thinking, if I had your cell phone number, maybe we could text over the weekend. It'll be more entertaining than a wedding reception for people I don't know."

Inside, I wanted to jump and shout for joy that he wanted my cell number. On the outside, I kept it calm and collected.

"Okay." I picked up my phone.

He smiled and pulled his phone from his pocket.

After the exchange of numbers he stood to leave. I felt the impending loss of his presence in the pit of my stomach, like his absence would leave me empty somehow. The feeling was so thoroughly stupid that I almost laughed at myself. As if after one day he was now vital to my existence. Ludicrous. But the longing was there, nonetheless.

Adrian's blue eyes locked on mine, narrowing slightly, perhaps measuring the emotion on my face. I hoped he couldn't see how much I dreaded his departure, since I had no way to explain the crazy feelings bubbling inside me.

Then all at once the dread lifted, eased, seemed to flow right out of my body, only to be replaced with a sense of assurance. Maybe Adrian wouldn't be like other guys who said they would call or text, but never really did. Suddenly, I had every confidence that he would contact me over the weekend. He wasn't just blowing smoke. He genuinely wanted to get to know me, and I could count on him.

How I knew these things I could not explain. I had no clue where the faith had come from. I only knew I had it. Adrian *would* text. He *would* call. I did not have to be afraid or alone.

"I'll be in touch," he whispered.

And I sat speechless, watching him walk down the road in the direction of his house.

CHAPTER 6

"Are you going to let me read the texts?" Viv asked, voice singing with excitement. She hadn't even said hello. Just ambushed me at the locker Monday morning and started in immediately on the fact that Adrian and I had been texting most of the weekend.

Because, yes, I'd texted her Friday night and told her about my Pre-Cal tutor, and the fact that he'd wanted my number. I remembered enough of my pre-family-crisis life to know that there was some sort of rule that said girls talked about boys. Although, Viv hadn't shared anything about Brett yet, but that was going to change in a matter of moments if I had anything to say about it.

"There's nothing scandalous or earth-shattering in there," I said. "Just a lot of stuff about helping Ms. Turner with the wedding cake, and a few things about his parents."

That much was the truth. We hadn't shared any great secrets during our text exchange, but Adrian had been quick with the replies and quite funny as he described the goings-on at the wedding reception. And he'd continued to text on Sunday after church. So even though I hadn't really learned any more about him – other than that he *did* keep his word – I'd become pretty comfortable talking to him.

"So where are his parents?"

Together, we turned to head for homeroom.

"Budapest," I answered, lowering my voice. I didn't want any of this overheard and making its way back to Nikki. She didn't need another reason to hate me. "His dad is teaching English over there."

"That's so exotic!"

"Let's talk about you and Brett Martin," I whispered, nudging her in the shoulder. "I saw you two in the hall on Friday. Why didn't you tell me you had something going on with him?"

"Because I'm not sure there is." Viv blushed a bright red and giggled. "But I really want there to be."

"When did this start?" I asked. Talking boys with Viv felt both good and weird. Good, because boy talk was normal and I'd had way too little normal lately. Weird, because part of me still felt I didn't deserve *normal*.

"A couple of weeks ago. We ran into each other at the community picnic and just started talking."

"Nice," I said, wiggling my eyebrows at her. "He's always seemed like a great guy."

"He is," she sighed, a dreamy smile on her face. "I keep hoping he'll ask me out, but he hasn't yet."

"He hasn't made any secret about your *friendship*," I said, emphasizing the last word. "He was smiling at you like a goofy kid the other day."

"And you spent the weekend texting with the hot new biker guy!"

As we neared our homeroom, I decided we should put a hold on the conversation. "Let's talk about this later. Don't want anybody overhearing all this girl talk." I nodded toward the group of kids gathered around the doorway.

Viv got the hint, and as we stepped into class all talk of boys ceased until a safer moment presented itself.

I dreaded talking to Mr. Austin about student government elections, but I knew I had to. After class, I forced myself to approach him.

He shuffled a stack of papers on his desk into a neat pile then closed them in a file folder. He looked up as he saw me approach, and I decided to just spit it out.

"I can't run for president again."

It was kind of like ripping a bandage off you skin all at once for the sake of getting it over with. It stung for a bit, but was better than prolonging the inevitable.

He nodded, like he'd been expecting it. "Care to tell me why?"

"Too soon," I said. "After everything, I just can't imagine being in the spotlight."

"I understand you need some time," he replied.

A lump formed in my throat, both because of Mr. Austin's kindness, and the fact that he had no idea exactly *why* I needed time.

"The deadline is in two weeks." He pointed toward the student government poster. "You've got some time to consider. Just give it some more thought."

I couldn't imagine a scenario when I'd feel comfortable in front of people, the way the class president role required, but I nodded anyway, because I didn't want Mr. Austin to be too disappointed.

Vivian hadn't waited for me. I'd told her to go on, since I needed a moment to talk to Mr. Austin. When I stepped into the hallway a few kids remained, wrapping things up before leaving for the day. One stop at my locker and I'd be ready to go.

"You sure weren't thinking about running for office when you met up with us that first time." Nikki's voice came from behind me, just as I was throwing my backpack over one shoulder. "Or the second or third time. All you cared about was getting smashed."

Apparently they'd eavesdropped on my conversation with Mr. Austin. Perfect. However, Nikki was sort of right. Maybe if I acknowledged that she'd go away.

"You're right." I shut my locker with more force than necessary. "I didn't care about anything but forgetting."

"And you were all too happy to let Nikki buy the liquor and drive you around," Courtney sneered.

Ironic, that Courtney would accuse me of taking advantage of Nikki, and all the resources her stinking rich horse-trainer dad could provide, when Courtney herself was the original coattail rider. The fact that Courtney was the daughter of a single mom who jumped from man to man and didn't care enough about herself or her daughter to stay clean and sober was not what made Courtney trashy. It was the way she super-glued herself to Nikki in order to maintain her social status. In the crazy, backwards way of obtaining popularity in high school, Courtney would've been nothing without Nikki.

On the other hand, Nikki was a real bitch who thought her rich parents could get her anything. Or *out* of anything. Like drunk driving charges.

"And wouldn't the voting public like to know that the class president spent the summer getting totally wasted?" And she just proved my point. "Maybe we should just let that secret out."

"If you listened in on my conversation with Mr. Austin, you already know I'm not running for president again," I said.

"Still it would be quite the scandal," Nikki suggested.

"Yeah." This from Courtney. She was *so* brilliant.

"Why do you two want to torture me over this?" I pushed away from my locker and stepped away. "I did not abandon you on purpose, but I'll be damned if I'm going to be sorry I escaped the fallout. Both of you would've done the same. Even if I'd gotten caught with you, you'd still be in the same trouble you are now. I wasn't driving. I didn't wreck the car, and I didn't have weed on me. That night was a wake-up call for me. It should be for you, too. The charges could've been even worse, or we could've all been dead."

"Whatever." Wow. Another intelligent response from Courtney. "You'll regret skipping out on us."

Time for this to end. And I would end it on my terms. I would have the last word this time.

"You drove drunk." I pointed at Nikki. "And you had marijuana in your purse." I pointed at Courtney. "Both of you just suck it up and deal with it. And leave me the hell alone."

Nikki was closest to me, so I shoved her hard with my shoulder as I pushed past, leaving them in the hall while I made my way to the front sidewalk.

My phone buzzed just as I caught sight of my mom in the line of cars. A text from Adrian. I clicked to open it.

Hey Zoe. You ok?

Glancing toward the parking lot, I saw him standing next to his motorcycle. Had he waited for me? Or worse, had he overheard the confrontation with Nikki and Courtney?

I texted back.

Fine.

I watched him read the message, and sent him a small wave when he looked back up at me. He nodded and smiled, and a sense of comfort flooded me. He seemed *so* familiar, like I'd known him for years? How did he happen to show up or text at just the right moments?

As Mom and I pulled out of the school, another text arrived.

Call me if Pre-Cal gives you trouble.

My heart did a flip in my chest.

Sure.

CHAPTER 7

I managed my homework with only a couple of texts to Adrian. I really wanted him to come over, Pre-Cal or no, but I didn't want to come across as desperate. I was also trying very hard to keep all things Adrian in the proper perspective.

Trying and failing miserably. Because the truth was, I was as taken with him as any girl had ever been with a boy.

Mom came home at her regular time and busied herself in the kitchen, while I sat on the couch with my cell phone, willing it to flash with an incoming text, and forcing myself to resist the urge to text him first.

On the mantle above the fireplace, the last family photo of my mom, dad, and me stared down at me. I rarely looked at it, instead choosing to forget about it. But in quiet moments like these, it was there, reminding me, mocking me, showing me all I'd lost, pointing out all my mistakes. On the lamp stand next to the sofa sat the only other picture of my dad still displayed in the house. I was four years old, and Dad and I were flying a kite together. Mom had removed the other pictures after the shit hit the fan, but she said she thought it was important to keep these two out, so that we wouldn't forget that things had once been very, very good.

Yeah right. All I was remembering these days were the last few months. And they'd sucked. Big time.

"Have you met Mrs. Turner's nephew?" Mom's voice interrupted my gloom and doom.

"Adrian?"

"Is that his name?" she asked. "I guess if you know that you must've met him."

I nodded. "He's helped me with my Pre-Cal homework."

"That's nice." Mom sat down on the couch with me, in that gesture that said she was about to open the lines of communication.

I stared at the aged blue upholstery of the sofa and resisted the urge to groan out loud. I did not want to have a heart to heart.

"I guess student government elections will be starting up soon," she said. "That ought to keep you busy for a while."

"I'm not running." Closing my eyes, I did my best to prepare for the onslaught of questions.

"Why not?"

"I don't want all that attention. I can't handle it right now." I still had not looked up from the couch cushions.

She didn't immediately respond. I heard her take a deep breath, like she was gathering thoughts with which to berate me. I turned my cell phone over and over in my hand, wishing it would ring and give me an excuse to stop this conversation. I just didn't have the ability to make small talk – or meaningful dialogue – with my mom.

"Zoe, you can't hide forever."

I didn't know why the hell not. I said nothing, hoping she'd get the hint that I didn't want to talk. No such luck.

"What happened with your father happened," she said. "And it was awful. But you have to go on with your life sweetheart."

I didn't want to do this. Didn't want to talk about this. Didn't want to argue with my mother. Could she please just leave it alone?

My non-response did not deter her. She plowed right on. "He'd want you to."

"Move on?" I snapped. "Maybe you can. You'd already separated. You'd already removed him from your life. I didn't get that luxury."

"Luxury?" Mom sounded incredulous. "Zoe, it wasn't..."

"Do you know how bad I wished I could divorce him the way you could?"

"We hadn't decided to divorce. We were just..."

But I didn't let her speak. I barreled on. "You have no idea what it's like to know that I wanted him gone from my life, but knowing I could never get rid of him. I *hated* him. I wished I'd never have to see him again! And then to have that actually happen?"

"Zoe, I'm so sorry." Maybe she was sorry for pushing the issue. Maybe she was just sorry about the shitstorm that had rained all over our family. Either way, it looked like she finally got the point.

"Don't lecture me about moving on with my life." I managed to lower my voice enough that I wasn't yelling anymore.

"I know this is complicated for you," Mom whispered. "I just want to help."

"Then just stay out of my head." I headed for the door.

"Where are you going?"

"For a walk." I said. "I need some space."

She didn't try to stop me.

I'd always been glad that the paddocks of Bryton Farms were an easy walk from my house. The sight of the horses calmed me. The earthy smell of the grass sometimes helped put things in perspective. I leaned against a fence, gazing out toward a beautiful chestnut stallion, wishing I could think of nothing besides the gentle giant now strolling in the field.

The exchange with my mom still loomed heavy in my mind, and putting space between us hadn't helped much. She wanted to help – I knew that – but I resented her interference just the same.

The rumble of a motor sounded in the distance. From the corner of my eye I caught sight of a shiny black motorcycle glinting as it topped a small rise in the road. Somehow I wasn't surprised. Just one more example of Adrian's uncanny ability to show up at the perfect time.

I stayed where I was, leaned against the fence, not even turning around as he pulled the bike to a stop. Happy as I was to see him, it wouldn't do to act too excited, because that would give too much away. Plus, excitement was just not in my mood profile at the moment.

Adrian said nothing as he approached, eventually leaning against the fence next to me. His presence moved over me like a soft blanket of calm, and I began to feel the tension ease from my body.

I wondered if he had any idea the effect he had on me?

"You like the horses?" he asked, voice soft and deep.

I shrugged. "I don't ride, but I like to watch them. They're calming."

"Upset?"

"Fight with my mom," I said. Then I corrected. "Not really a fight. More of a discussion she wanted that I refused to have."

He nodded, as if he knew I didn't need advice. In that moment, it was his silent understanding that caused me to open the floodgates.

"My dad had an affair," I said.

CHAPTER 8

I f Adrian was shocked or surprised by my blurting out about my dad's infidelity, he didn't show it. He just stayed where he was, leaned against the fence, looking at me not with pity, but with a kind of understanding and compassion I couldn't comprehend.

"He came clean to my mom back in the spring," I said. Now that I'd cracked the ice, I figured why not let loose with all my baggage and drama. "A few weeks later they decided to do a trial separation and marriage counseling. That's when they told me."

He leaned closer. "Must've been hard on you."

"I was so angry." I turned my head from the horse and looked at Adrian. "I still am. In my mind, he'd betrayed me as much as he had my mom. We were a family. He was supposed to protect us, not tear us apart."

"You're absolutely right," Adrian whispered, his voice sliding over me with so much serenity that I felt complete confidence and comfort in sharing the deepest, darkest part of my life with him.

The breeze picked up, cutting through the heat of the August evening. The soft touch of the wind encouraged me to keep going.

"They just sat me down at the kitchen table, like we were going to talk about where to go on vacation or something, but instead they destroyed my life. I was devastated. Too devastated to even cry. I just sat there staring at the tabletop. I knew they expected a response, but all I could think was how much I hated him at that moment. So that's what I told him."

"I'm sure you felt that way at the time."

I couldn't begin to put into words what it meant to me at that moment, to have someone just listen, and not try convince me that I'd overreacted, or try to persuade me to move on. Adrian just let me talk. And so far, no one else had done that.

Which was why I'd just stopped talking about it.

"I did," I replied. "And for a long time after. Or it seemed like a long time anyway. In my mind, I knew I should regret what I'd said, but I just couldn't make myself feel it. My dad kept trying to reconnect with me, even after he'd moved out. He'd call, but I'd refuse to talk to him. When he came by the house again I was just as nasty to him."

Part of me wondered what in the world I was doing, unloading everything I'd been holding inside onto someone who was pretty much a complete stranger. But then Adrian's calming presence wrapped around me, and my misgivings didn't matter. Sometimes it was easier to confide in a stranger anyway.

"The first week of summer vacation, my dad died in a car wreck."

He let out a heavy sigh and reached over to take my hand, his touch light and sweet. He said nothing. I was thankful again for his silent understanding.

"He was coming home from Cincinnati. It was raining. A pick-up truck hydroplaned and hit him."

"And you were left with everything unresolved." He squeezed my hand.

I nodded. "I feel guilty for that. And now, for the first time, I'm starting to miss my dad. But that doesn't make the anger go away."

"Let's go for a ride." He inclined his head toward the bike.

My insides lit up like a Christmas tree, bright and sparkling. I hadn't felt that kind of energy in months. Me, on a bike with Adrian, forced to hold onto him? Yes, yes, and yes. It was almost enough to make me forget.

I fought for control of my enthusiasm. I didn't want to appear over-eager. Glancing at his bike, then back at him, I said, "You only have one helmet."

"I have a spare at the house." His hand still holding mine, he walked us toward the motorcycle. "You can have this one for now, and I'll stop at home and get the other."

He handed me the helmet and I stared, not exactly sure how to put it on.

Adrian solved the problem. He took the helmet, slipped it on my head, and secured the strap beneath my chin. For a split second I wondered how ridiculous I looked, then decided I didn't care.

He hopped on the bike and looked back at me. "You're not scared are you?"

Scared? No. Unsure? A bit. But not enough to chicken out. Heart pounding, I climbed on behind him. He reached for both my hands, pulled my arms around his middle. The effect was instant and intense. Pressed against him like this, worry, stress, guilt, grief – they all just melted away.

"Hold on," he said, and then turned to crank the bike.

I sighed. Like I'd want to do anything else.

Stopping at Ms. Turner's house, Adrian went to the garage to get his spare helmet, and I texted my mom. With a quick apology, I told her I was with Adrian and would be home soon. I didn't wait for a response before shutting my phone off and sticking it back in my pocket.

Adrian was back in less than a minute with a black helmet identical to the one he'd let me wear.

Mrs. Turned must've heard us, because she stepped out the front door.

"Hi there, Zoe," she called from the porch.

I waved. "Hello Mrs. Turner."

"Zoe's going to show me the town, Aunt Maggie," Adrian said. "From a teenager's perspective."

Mrs. Turner laughed. "I'm sure that'll be interesting. Have fun and be careful."

With a final wave, she disappeared back into the house.

Adrian turned toward me, slipping the helmet over his head. I didn't know a lot about motorcycles, but his looked new.

"What kind of bike is this?" I asked.

"It's a Suzuki Boulevard," he answered, adjusting the chinstrap.

"Is it new?"

"Yeah." He swung his leg over the seat and motioned for me to climb on behind him. "It was a present from my parents for my eighteenth birthday."

"You're already eighteen?" I don't know why the thought surprised me so much. He already seemed so much more mature than any of the other guys my age.

"August second," he said, cranking the ignition. "When do you turn eighteen?"

"December eleventh."

"So I'm only four months older." He turned his head and grinned before rolling the motorcycle back onto Stableview Road.

I settled in behind him, arms around him, soaking in his strength as he effortlessly guided the bike to the bank of the creek that ran below his aunt's property. The air moved against my skin like velvet, magnifying the warmth that spread from Adrian and into me. The blacktop wound and flowed with the hills, until I felt like we were somehow one with the road.

Adrian maneuvered the bike off Stableview Road and onto the main highway, pointing it in the direction of the town. In a matter of minutes, we rolled into the city limits.

"So tell me about Rison," he said, turning his head slightly so I could hear him.

I leaned my head further over his shoulder and rested my chin there. "The usual stuff. Banks. Library. Courthouse."

"That's it?" he asked, slowing the motorcycle as we drove down Main Street. "What about that coffee shop over there?"

"That's a new place," I answered. "Seems to be a nice addition to the town. Not a lot of kids hang out there, though, because they're only open during regular business hours. Plus it's always full of people that work downtown."

"Where do kids our age usually hang out?"

"The pizza restaurant over close to school," I said. Releasing my hold on him long enough to gesture to the right side of the road, I continued. "Or the sandwich shop up there on the corner."

"Maybe we'll have to hit one of those places sometime," Adrian said, making a loop through a parking lot and heading us back through town. "You can introduce me to the social scene of Rison."

The thought had me smiling, even though I didn't know when – if *ever* – I'd be ready to step out into that type of activity again. For now, it was nice to know that Adrian liked the idea of hanging out with me.

He turned back onto Stableview Road, and I figured he was taking me home. But just before a sharp left turn would've taken us in the direction of our houses, Adrian pulled the motorcycle onto a wide gravel shoulder.

Cutting the engine, he took off his helmet and turned around. "Hope you don't mind a short walk."

I shook my head, reaching up to undo the strap of my helmet.

He helped me off the bike and took my hand again, walking toward the peaceful sound of trickling water.

Two minutes later, after a short trek through the thick trees, we arrived at a clearing – a flat, grassy expanse of land right at the edge of the water. It was beautiful, like a hidden oasis in the middle of the little nowhere that was Rison. I could picture long moments hiding out here.

"It's a peaceful spot," Adrian said. "An escape, but not too far from home. I thought you might like it."

"It's amazing." I kicked off my sandals and bent to roll up my jeans. "I know you're getting rid of those biker boots to go wading with me."

Without missing a beat, he knelt to untie his boots, shooting me a smile that reached right inside and squeezed my heart.

The rocky bed of the creek contrasted sharply with the soft grass from the bank, but the cool water and smooth rocks felt divine under my feet. I welcomed the awareness of the world around me. I'd had too little of that lately.

"Sometimes just connecting with nature helps," Adrian said. Again, I wondered if he'd somehow read my thoughts.

"It does," I agreed.

We'd walked only a few yards from where we left our shoes, but I already felt better, lighter, and not quite so burdened. I couldn't explain Adrian's effect on me. I only knew it existed.

"Thank you for bringing me here," I said.

"My pleasure."

I stopped walking and turned to him. "But I'm sort of confused."

"Why?" He seemed genuinely puzzled.

"I guess I'm just wondering about all this attention," I began. "You show up to help me with my homework just when I'm about to give up. You text me just when I need a reason to smile. You find me on the side of the road after a fight with my mom. All these things happening during what's probably the worst time in my whole life. It's like you showed up here in Rison just for me, and I know that can't be true."

He narrowed his eyes and half-smiled, but said nothing.

"Why are you paying so much attention to me?" There, I said it. Just put it all out there.

"Is it that hard to believe that I'm interested?" He reached for my hand, pulled me closer to him. "That I want to get to know you?"

Inside my chest my heart hammered and I could hear the blood rushing through my veins. The nearness of him and the sincerity in his voice made it difficult to breathe.

He took my free hand and threaded our fingers together, using both hands to pull closer, until I was almost flush against him. Tilting my head, I found his baby blues locked on me. The sun had begun its descent behind the trees as dusk settled, the sky glowing a warm orange.

"I've got a lot of baggage," I whispered. "I'm practically a basket case."

He raised one shoulder in a casual shrug.

"Why me?" I hated that I still needed reassurance.

"I found what I was looking for when I saw you."

And just like that my world shifted, tilted on its axis. My chest tightened with emotions so foreign, so intense, their beauty almost painful. The cool water swirled around my ankles as I shifted, trying to rebalance myself and not crumple at his feet.

Adrian was a man of few words, and his few words had slain me.

"I can't claim to understand how you feel," he said, squeezing my hands. "And I won't always have the answers. But I can listen. And I can care. All the time."

Staring up at him, I could not find the words to express the feelings bubbling inside. He didn't seem to mind my silence. His eyes stayed glued on mine, a sweet smile playing across his face.

"Okay," I whispered. It was the best I could come up with.

He wrapped his arms around me and kissed the top of my head. I figured he could probably feel my heart pounding against his chest. I hugged him back, giving myself over to the crazy wonderful sensation of being in his arms.

"We better get you home," he said after a long moment. "Don't want your mom mad at me already."

Hand in hand, we stepped out of the water and up onto the creek bank. Everything felt so perfect.

I was almost afraid to wonder might happen next.

CHAPTER 9

The following morning Mom was full of questions.

"Are you going to tell me what you did last night?" she asked. I could hear the suspicion in her voice.

"Nothing really," I said, hoping to avoid the conversation altogether.

But, no.

"Forgive me if I don't think that's an acceptable explanation," Mom said. "Especially considering how you spent your summer."

"Seriously, Mom?" I let the sarcasm ring from my voice, not really caring that I was taking her bait. "Do you want me to tell you I was out drinking and smoking pot with Nikki and Courtney?"

Walking away from her, I grabbed my backpack from the couch and walked toward the front door.

"Of course not, Zoe." I heard her keys jingle as she grabbed them from the coffee table. "But it's not unreasonable for a mother to expect to know how her teenage daughter spent the evening."

I opened the front door, stared out toward the road, and ignored her.

She didn't let up. "I didn't ask you last night because I didn't want to start an argument. Obviously, you weren't out late, and I know Mrs. Turner's nephew dropped you off at home. I thought maybe this morning you'd be more receptive to the idea of having a conversation with me."

She was in one of those moods where she wouldn't let up. I figured I might as well finish it so we could get on with our day.

"There's nothing to tell you, Mom," I said, my voice snarky as I turned to face her. "I was pissed at you for trying to make me talk about Dad, so I walked down toward the paddocks. Adrian drove by and saw me. He stopped to say hi then offered me a ride on the motorcycle. He said he wanted to know about Rison, so we drove into town, I showed him what little there is to see, and then we drove back. End of story."

Without waiting for a response, I turned back around and headed to the car. I'd intentionally left out the part about the clearing. That memory was mine, and I wasn't about to share it.

"You rode a motorcycle with a boy you just met?" She sounded shocked.

"Yes, I did," I said, sliding into the passenger seat. "And you'll be happy to know he was sober and a much safer driver than the last classmate I rode around with."

I slammed my door for emphasis.

Mom got in, started the car, and didn't say another word as we drove to school.

All day at school Adrian was attentive. Not so much that it drew a lot of attention, but enough that I noticed. I kept an eye out for Nikki and Courtney, hoping they weren't stalking me enough to realize that Adrian and I had a connection. Everything was fine until lunch.

Adrian's lunch period overlapped mine by ten minutes. When Viv and I walked in, he was seated at a table near the backdoor with Daniel Williams, a computer-whiz who'd also been on student government with me the previous year.

Adrian must've been watching for me, because as soon as Viv and I stepped into the cafeteria, he waved us over. There was no way I could say no, nor did I want to. But as we took off in the direction of Adrian and Daniel's table, I noticed Nikki at the door we'd just come through.

The icy glare in her eyes told me she'd seen Adrian's wave.

As much as I didn't want her revenge-radar aimed at me, if she was pissed because Adrian liked me and not her, she could just deal with it.

I dropped into the seat next to him while Viv went on to the sandwich bar.

"Do good on your Pre-Cal homework?" he asked, a grin tugging the corners of his mouth. He knew good and well I'd done fine. He'd gotten me through it with a few helpful texts.

"Of course," I said. "It was a piece of cake."

From across the way, Viv caught my eye. She tilted her head to the right. Looking that direction I saw Nikki headed straight for us. Clearly, she was on a mission. Her fuchsia-streaked hair bounced with every purposeful step.

I had maybe two seconds to brace myself.

"How nice that you're making friends, Adrian." Contempt dripped from her voice and pooled around us like motor oil leaking from an engine, slimy and unwanted.

Adrian slipped his arm along the back of my seat and leaned close. "I think so."

"Watch this one." Nikki threw a hand on one hip and turned toward me. "She had a wild summer."

Behind me, I felt the muscles in Adrian's arm tense. Slowly, deliberately I stood so that I was face to face with Nikki.

"I know you want to blame me for what happened that night," I began, dropping my voice to a whisper so the nosey people around wouldn't get an earful. "And yes, I was drunk. But I did not crash the car and I did not have pot in my purse. That's on you and Courtney. I still have no idea how I got out of the car, but you have to know that the two of you would've still gotten hauled away by the police even if I'd been there."

Nikki's eyes narrowed, darts of anger aimed at me. "But you would've been hauled off with us."

I took a deep breath, trying to remain calm. She was right. I would've been sitting in the police station just like the two of them if I hadn't somehow escaped.

"You're right. I would've been." I figured I could give her that. "But the charges against me wouldn't have been DUI or possession of marijuana."

"Bitch." She shoved my shoulder, hard enough that the backs of my legs knocked into the chair and created a commotion.

Steadying myself, I prepared to come right back at her. But Adrian stood up and stepped between us, coming to my rescue yet again.

"Enough," he said, his quiet strength stopping the confrontation in its tracks.

Turning to me, he pointed to Nikki and said, "She's not worth getting in trouble for."

And then to Nikki. "If Zoe took that incident as a sign that she was heading in the wrong direction and needed to straighten up, who are you to deny her that?"

Surprise crossed Nikki's face, just as fear spread through my heart.

"You know?" I whispered.

He looked at me, no scorn or judgment in his eyes. Shrugging his shoulders, he said. "Small school." Then, leaning closer, he said beneath his voice. "Don't worry. It's not common knowledge."

"When?" Had he known last night when we waded in the creek together?

Nikki took the hint and left, thank the lord.

"I overheard Courtney on the phone. I figure she was talking to Nikki. I didn't get a lot of details, but I heard your name. And after our talk last night, I just sort of put two and two together. You had a lousy summer. Makes sense you might've made some bad decisions."

My stomach pitched with waves of embarrassment. Not that I wouldn't have eventually told Adrian. I would've confided in him sooner rather than later. After all, I'd already shared one big chunk of baggage with him. But it would've been on my terms. Not this way, with Nikki spilling my worst mistake in the middle of school lunchroom.

"It's okay," he whispered, taking my hand.

Calming energy seemed to flow from his hand into mine, spreading through my whole body with warmth and peace. The feeling of shame began to drift away, leaving behind a sense of new beginnings.

"I'm not here to judge you," he said, his thumb tracing circles on the back of my hand. "You're not the first teenager to screw up, and you won't be the last. The important thing is to learn from it and move on."

Viv returned with her lunch, looking at me tentatively. She knew enough to know there was bad blood between Nikki and me, but she didn't know the extent of it. I'd tell her, of course. Today. First chance I got.

"It's okay," I mouthed to her, and she, Adrian, and I sat down at the table.

As if by unspoken agreement, Adrian put a hold on our conversation. His hand settled with soothing warmth

on my shoulder, and all the tension from the confrontation with Nikki ebbed away.

He left a moment later, headed to his Pre-Cal class. I
carried on a lively conversation with Viv as she finished
her lunch, but didn't eat. I had no appetite.

I knew Adrian's words were true. And I knew I'd
moved on from the heavy partying and drinking. But the
feelings that drove me to those things still simmered
inside. All the anger and guilt.

I wondered how he would react if he knew.

CHAPTER 10

"I almost told you last night," I said as we shut our Pre-Cal books, homework finished. The warm afternoon humidity simmered around the picnic table where we worked. "And I would've told you myself. It's important to me that you know that."

Adrian just smiled. "I know, Zoe. And I would've let you tell me and pretended I hadn't figured it out already. But I couldn't let that confrontation go on any longer."

His sense of protectiveness astounded me. I owed him the details of that night, if only so that he could hear the truth from me.

I turned so I sat facing him on the bench, thankful for the slight breeze now stirring the air.

"We were coming back from Lexington. We'd all been drinking. I was really gone. Nikki was driving. God, we were idiots." I shook my head, marveling at my own stupidity. But I'd come this far. I wouldn't hold back now.

"We met a cop. Nikki turned off on a side road to try and out run him. When he turned to follow us she shut off the car lights." Adrian reached for both my hands. I took a deep breath and went on. "I remember the crash.

We hit something. A ditch or a tree, I'm not sure. I slid all over the backseat and hit my head when we slammed into whatever it was. I was totally disoriented then. I remember thinking this was really bad, but not remembering why. I heard the sirens in the distance, and I knew something big was about to hit the fan. I remember thinking I should try to get up, but…"

It was then I remembered the strange sensation of arms around me, lifting me from the car and flying away with me. Closing my eyes, the sense of comfort I'd felt in those moments surrounded me once again. I thought it was probably best to leave out that strange hallucination.

"The next thing I knew, I woke up in my bed." I had a momentary flash of the boy I'd imagined in my room that morning, but shoved it away, wanting to get through the rest of the story. I stared down at our joined hands and kept talking. "It was early. The house was quiet, so I knew my mom wasn't up yet. And it was still kind of dark. I couldn't remember how I'd gotten home. I still don't. I guess I must've gotten out of the car somehow and walked. But we were probably three miles from here when we wrecked. It's crazy to think I walked that far, but it's the only logical explanation."

I looked up at him then. I don't know what I'd been expecting to see, but the genuine care beaming from his expression just about did me in.

"A little later when my mom came in, I realized somehow I'd gotten home without getting arrested. That's when I decided I had to stop the destructive behavior. It was bad enough that we were all smashed and we could've all been killed in that car crash. But when I thought about what could've happened to me on that walk home? A drunk girl all alone wandering the countryside?"

He leaned his forehead to mine, his skin soft and warm, and just looked at me with a smile on his face. It seemed he was waiting for me to smile back, so I did.

That's when he spoke. "I'm really glad nothing bad happened to you that night."

The whisper of his voice echoed in my heart, and for the first time in a very long time I felt like something other than an ungrateful brat who'd killed my father with my hate.

At the thought of my father, a tear escaped and rolled down my cheek. Adrian's thumb swept it away, his hand settling gently against my face.

My chest expanded until I thought it might explode as Adrian shifted his head slightly and leaned closer. The split second before his lips touched mine seemed like a million years, and in those million years all kinds of thoughts raced through my brain.

I'd just told him the story of my horrible, stupid mistake, and his reaction is to kiss me? Was it a pity kiss? Was it some kind of show of sympathy? Would I embarrass myself with lack of technique or excess slobber?

Then he kissed me, and every thought I'd been thinking fled. Nothing else existed except this. *This.* Softness and heat meshed together. But even in the midst of it, I knew it was so much more than that.

It was what all that softness and heat represented. It was the way my heart filled and overflowed, in a way I'd thought was lost to me forever. It was the reality of his presence in my life.

He didn't manhandle me. Not even close. Tenderness emanated from him as he molded his mouth to mine. I was absolutely lost.

I couldn't breathe.

I couldn't think.

I didn't want to.

After a long, sweet moment, he pulled away, just enough that his lips still grazed mine as he said, "Really glad."

I must've looked confused, because he quickly added, "That you made it through that night unharmed."

"Guess I had a guardian angel or something," I said, our faces still pressed close, breath still mingling.

He chuckled. "Or something."

"Can I tell you a secret?" I whispered.

He tucked a strand of hair behind my ear, his fingers lingering on my cheek. "Of course."

"It didn't help." I leaned back a bit, enough to look him in the eye. "The drinking and the partying. I thought it did, and I guess for a few minutes when I was wasted and numb, I forgot a little bit. But not really."

He slid his hand to the back of my neck and squeezed, pressing a soft kiss to my forehead. He seemed to have an uncanny knack of knowing when I didn't need him to say anything.

"I wanted it to help. Was desperate for it to help. But it didn't. I still felt awful." I closed my eyes, the shame of my next words sitting on my chest like a thousand Pre-Cal textbooks. "I still feel awful."

CHAPTER 11

A week had passed since the episode with Nikki in the cafeteria. Thankfully, she'd given Adrian and me a wide berth since, and even though I knew she'd come back at me eventually, I was glad for the reprieve.

There'd also been no talk of my dad or my foolish behavior over the summer. Admitting it all to Adrian hadn't been that difficult, but it still left me pretty raw, and he must've realized I needed some time before the subject came up again.

The idea that Adrian must be able to read minds popped up again, and made me smile.

Sitting at the picnic table in my backyard, I tilted my head into the light breeze that cooled my skin. The afternoon was uncharacteristically pleasant for late August, which meant as Adrian walked to my house for our homework session, he was not roasting in the sun.

Pre-Cal homework had become our standing date. Weird, but nice. And pretty special.

And given that I was still on a short leash with my mom, it was the kind of date she couldn't object to.

I caught sight of him as he rounded the curve just shy of my driveway. He looked almost surreal, like some kind of angel descending into my life, not just a friendly neighbor walking down the road.

Yesterday during our homework session, he'd encouraged me to think about running for student government. I resisted the idea, but the more I'd thought about his logic, the more sense it made. He said I shouldn't let my dad's bad judgment or the tragedy that took his life keep me from doing the things I enjoyed. He said that would be like letting the bad guys win. It was still difficult to imagine myself in the role of class president, but maybe I could find a happy medium.

"You look like someone with a secret," he said, striding to the picnic table and taking a seat beside me.

I felt like I had a secret. Sitting here each afternoon with Adrian, as I'd been for the past week, I felt like I'd found some kind of treasure no one else knew about. Whatever it was that was budding between us, it was the most delicious secret of my life.

"I think I'm going to run for student government."

He scooted closer and leaned in to kiss my cheek. "I'm glad."

"But not for president." The warmth of his kiss stayed on my skin, and I smiled. "Maybe for reporter or secretary. Something a little more low-key. I'll tell Mr. Austin tomorrow."

"Great idea." He took my hand in both of his. "Can I tell you something?"

"Sure." So much of the time our conversations wound up centering on me and my neuroses, but I never wanted him to feel like this relationship – or whatever it was – was all one-sided. "You can tell me anything."

"I'm happy." He tilted his head, his baby blues locking on mine. "Really happy. I didn't expect that when I came here."

I couldn't have stopped the huge grin that spread across my face if someone had offered me a million dollars.

"You like that?" he asked, a mischievous glint in his eyes.

"Yeah." I couldn't suppress the giggle. "The idea that I could make someone happy. Make *you* happy. I like that idea."

The truth was, I'd given my family and friends so much grief over the past few months I'd forgotten what it felt like to actually do something positive for another person. Selfishness was a dark pit, and it was nice to think maybe I was climbing my way out.

"Not just happy," he whispered, pressing his forehead to mine. "Really happy."

My only response was a heavy sigh. I had no words. None.

"I figured coming here would be like anything else, just something I needed to do. Finish high school. Hang out with Aunt Maggie. I didn't expect this. You."

This close, I could feel his breath on my cheek. I caught the minty scent of toothpaste.

He leaned in even closer, his lips moving against my cheek.

"Zoe?"

"Hmmm?" Coherency was not possible at the moment.

"I'm really, *really* happy."

He kissed me then, and holy cow! Happiness I didn't deserve took root in my heart, blooming brightly in every corner of my soul. His arms came around me, wrapping me in the sweet serenity his presence had come to represent, and yet there was so much more.

He was excitement and expectation and, yes... let's face it... passion. No denying it. The passion was definitely there. At least on my side of things.

And if the way he pulled me closer, held me tighter, and amped up the intensity of the kiss was any indication, it was there for him, too.

How crazy was that? That I could inspire a response like this from a guy who could've had any girl he wanted.

I felt his reluctance as he pulled away. Felt my own reluctance in the pit of my stomach.

"Homework," he managed, our faces still pressed together.

I nodded. He was right, but the reminder was pretty unwelcome at the moment.

With one arm, he reached around me for the Pre-Cal book, his other arm keeping me tight against him.

He kissed me once more, quick and soft, as he opened the book and picked up a pencil.

"I probably ought to meet your mom," he said as we both moved to give our attention to our homework. "She'd probably like to meet the guy who's nuts about her daughter."

CHAPTER 12

I was still awake long after I heard my mom turn in for the night. Lying in the bed, my mind kept returning to Adrian and our afternoon together. He'd quickly become such an important part of my life, and apparently, he felt the same.

Enough that he wanted to meet my mom.

Things we so strained between Mom and me that I had no idea how to even bring it up. It would be pretty awkward to just come right out with it after months of practically no meaningful communication between the two of us.

Hey Mom, I'm still really pissed about all that crap with Dad, and I don't want to talk about it with you, but hey, I met a guy.

Somehow I just didn't think that was the right way to approach it.

For a split second I wondered if my dad would like Adrian, or if he'd be like most dads were about the guys who dated their teenage daughters. A wave of sadness swept over me when that errant thought brought home all over again that my dad was gone forever.

Taking a deep breath, I nestled further into my pillow and pulled the blanket up over my shoulders. I could feel the first moments of slumber sliding toward me and welcomed them and the brief escape they offered.

Sleep claimed me, and in that dreamy place the scene began to change before my eyes.

Beyond the gray, hazy fog, the Rison Town Cemetery sloped with the gentle hills on which it sat. The lack of sunlight increased the creepy vibe the place gave off. My feet took me in that direction, even though my mind argued bitterly against it.

I hadn't been here since the day we buried him, and I couldn't figure out why I'd chosen such an eerie day to make my first visit.

The words ricocheted around in my head as I walked in the direction of his grave. All the things I wanted to say – things I should've said when he was still alive – clamored for attention. I wanted so badly to hate him forever. It would be easier that way. But somewhere along the way, after putting my father in the ground, the feelings of love that had once been so natural came seeping back into my heart.

His headstone was simple. *Jason Gray. Beloved Husband and Father. 1969 – 2013*. I almost laughed at the beloved husband part. Almost. Then I remembered why I was here.

I sank to my knees, unbothered by the damp ground beneath me. And in the quiet, mist-filled morning, I started to cry.

And the words rolled right out of me.

"I'm sorry, Daddy. So sorry. I don't hate you. I never did. I wanted to, but just because I was so mad at you for hurting Mom and screwing up our family. I guess I'm still mad. But I can't stop loving you, Dad. And I miss you so much."

Dragging the back of my hands across my cheeks, I cleared the tears from my eyes and looked up.

Somehow, he was there. My Dad. A cloudy, translucent vision of him, standing behind the headstone. His empty eyes stared through me, as if I wasn't even there.

"Daddy." My voice broke, but I continued, and said what I'd come here to say. "Can you forgive me?"

Without moving his eyes to look at me, and with zero emotion in his voice, he replied, "It's too late."

His image began to fade into the haze. Stumbling to my feet, I tried to reach him before he vanished.

"No, Daddy," I wailed, the misery welling inside me too overwhelming to bear. "Please!"

But he was gone.

Collapsing to the ground, I let despair overtake me, sobbing there beside my father's headstone.

I felt awareness begin to return, not in an upright bolt the way I might've after a nightmare, but in a slow trickle, that amplified the sadness and carried it from my dream into my consciousness.

In that moment, the weight of my grief choked me from the inside.

Cool wetness dampened my cheeks, and as I reached up to wipe my tears I opened my eyes, hoping that the sight of the real world would calm the emotions whirling in my soul.

And Adrian was there. On my lavender beanbag. Arms propped on knees covered by frayed blue jeans. Black tee shirt that matched his hair. His face etched with concern and compassion... and a barely caged anger.

What the —

I blinked, clearing away the moisture in my eyes for a better look.

But there was no one on my beanbag. I was alone.

I didn't imagine him. I hadn't even been thinking of him. So how had my mind conjured him there in my bedroom?

A crazy sense of déjà vu swept over me, and my mind flashed back to the morning after the crash. Waking up to the nasty effects of the night before, and hallucinating a guy sitting on my beanbag.

In my mind I pictured the vision from that morning. Blue jeans. Black hair. Biker boots.

Adrian.

It wasn't possible. The idea was absurd. And yet...

How often had I thought about how familiar he seemed, how familiar it *felt* to be with him? How many times had I asked myself since meeting him how he had the ability to show up or call or text at *just* the right moments? He saw me searching for my Pre-Cal book, and somehow it mysteriously appeared. Without asking he knew I'd need help with Pre-Cal homework. He texted to check on me just after a confrontation with Nikki and Courtney. He found me at the horse paddocks after a near fight with mom.

Then there's the way that when I'm with him, his presence wraps around me like warm breeze.

And now I was almost certain it had been him in my bedroom the morning of the hangover from hell. And there was no way I'd placed him there with some sort of wishful thinking. I hadn't even laid eyes on him yet.

Something was definitely weird about Adrian Shaw. Probably not in a bad way. At least I hoped. But something weird for sure.

CHAPTER 13

I dragged into school that morning, eyelids already drooping from the energy it had taken to get ready.

Sleep had eluded me after the horrible dream about my father. I just kept playing it over and over again in my mind, wondering if it was my dad's way of telling me he'd be pissed at me for all eternity.

Or if it was a manifestation of my own fears that I'd never be able to move on.

And in the moments when I wasn't reliving the dream, I'd think about Adrian randomly appearing in my bedroom, twice, and all the questions I had about exactly who and *what* he was.

I'd ask him. Though our relationship was still new, I figured we had enough trust between us that I could tell him what I'd seen, what I suspected, and maybe he wouldn't run screaming in the opposite direction of the insane girl he'd made the mistake of getting involved with.

Adrian, you've magically appeared my bedroom a couple of times, and I'm beginning to think maybe you have some really cool supernatural abilities. Am I right?

Yeah, it wasn't a conversation I was really looking forward to having. But honestly, I had enough crap to deal with without wondering if these hallucinations meant I was losing my mind.

I'd talk to him after school, when Pre-Cal homework was done.

In the lobby, my mood perked up a bit when I saw the signs Vivian had made for my run for senior class secretary hanging beside the office. The vivid blue and purple colors hung in bright contrast on the industrial white walls.

I'd told Viv the truth about the accident. She'd been glad I wasn't hurt, but she hadn't been shocked. She said she was glad I'd had good reason to cut ties with Nikki and Courtney.

In the hallway on the way to homeroom, I ran into Daniel and several other friends who'd served in student government with me.

"So glad you changed your mind and decided to run," Daniel said. "Even if it's not for president."

"You'll make a great president," I said. "I'm glad you're running. I really hope you get elected."

"Thanks," Daniel replied. "And it's cool you're running unopposed."

I still wasn't sure why no one had run against me, but I wasn't going to complain. I wasn't like I was in any shape to do heavy campaigning.

Carla Mabry, Andrea Bishop, and Nick Henry joined us, and congratulated me too. All of them were on the ballot for offices as well. Nick was the only one who hadn't served on student government before, but he was a nice guy and a really good student. He'd be a great student leader.

It felt good to be back in a familiar situation, with familiar friends who'd been with me for the past three years.

Viv walked up and smiled brightly, Brett standing right beside her.

"Thanks for the making the signs, Viv," I said, leaning over to give her a hug. "And thanks for forgiving me."

"Always here for you," she said, hugging me back. "You know that."

And I did know that. I hadn't told her about my dad's infidelity yet. Not because I didn't trust her, but because it was so humiliating, even though I knew she wouldn't look at me any differently. It was time to get past my embarrassment and tell her all of it. I wanted her to truly understand what had sent me spiraling out of control over the summer.

In the midst of the discussion, I saw Adrian halfway up the hallway, but the crowd of people between us kept me from being able to get to him. With a wave and a smile, he turned to head to his homeroom.

A tap on my shoulder drew my attention away from Daniel, Viv, and the others. Turning slightly, I found Courtney, without Nikki for once, standing behind me.

"I'm so glad you've decided to run for class secretary," she said. "Aren't you guys? I mean, she's just done so much for our school and we should all be so grateful for her service."

Since her interaction with this particular group of people was so out of character, Daniel and the rest of the gang just looked at her and said nothing, completely unsure how to respond.

"It's just so brave of you to step back into the spotlight after that nasty little business with your dad." She raised her voice, making sure she could be heard above the buzz in the hall.

"Courtney, shut up," I ordered. There was no way she could know what had happened.

"But why? I just want everyone to see how terrific you are." Sarcasm laced her words, and a crowd started to gather. The audience spurred her on.

"Messy stuff, when your dad leaves your mom for another woman. Especially the mom of one of your classmates. My mom was devastated when he died. They had such plans to be happy together. Just think Zoe, we could've been sisters."

Her words punched me in the gut. I felt their effect as if I'd been hammered with a baseball bat. The lights in the hallway suddenly seemed far too bright, and the figures of the people around me began to swim.

My head pounded, and my knees threatened to give way. Chaos erupted all around me. I was vaguely aware of people saying my name, shouting at Courtney, but my brain had gone into self-preservation mode.

Shut out the bad stuff. Shut out the bad stuff. Don't think about it now. Save it for later. Just get away. Just get away.

Pushing through a doorway just as the bell rang, I ran up the hall, no particular destination in mind. I found myself in the girls' bathroom at the end of the senior hallway. I was alone, thank God.

Outside the bathroom door I heard the last few people scuffling to class, hoping their tardiness would be overlooked. I didn't move. At that moment I could not have cared less about getting to homeroom.

Humiliation crashed over me, the emotion as violent as a tidal wave. My stomach pitched and rolled, and every breath caused my chest to ache. Darting my eyes around the empty restroom I noticed the back corner, between the sink and the window, and decided it was the perfect spot.

I slid my body into the corner and sank, dropping my backpack to the white tiled floor on the way down.

My dad had slept with Courtney's mom.

Courtney's mom who was a trashy, bed-hopping pill-popper.

Somehow I'd thought he'd had better taste in women than that.

Of course, when a guy decided to screw around on his wife, good judgment and taste went down the toilet.

My brain snapped into action. Courtney could be lying. She and Nikki were just looking for a way to get back at me. It could all be fabricated.

But how could she have known about the affair? Everyone knew my dad had died, but no one knew about the cheating. I hadn't told anyone. Not even Viv.

But I had told Adrian.

No, no, no! Adrian would not do this to me. He would not hurt me this way.

It was completely unfair that my dad wasn't here for me to scream at. Every bit of this was his fault. All the questions, lies, embarrassment. All of it.

God, Dad! You've totally ruined everything! I'm so messed up, so scared, so humiliated. You should be here so I could yell and scream and blame you. You should be here to help me with my math. You should be here so I could apologize for being so awful to you the last time we talked. You should be here.

Fog seemed to fill the room, seeping into every available space and pressing into me as if it were alive. The air turned humid and a dank smell filled my nostrils. Through the murkiness, the hazy figure of my dad appeared. Leaned against the doorway, arms crossed over his chest, he watched me with something almost giddy in his eyes.

My heart surged with an odd combination of joy and dread. Something was terribly wrong. How could he look happy while I sat in the floor of the school bathroom and grieved for him and all we'd lost?

I thought of my dream, of the way he hadn't even looked at me when he told me it was too late. Could it be that the damage could not be undone?

"Daddy." The whispered word scalded my throat as I said it. In those two syllables lived every fear, every regret, and every hope I possessed. Surely he would take pity on me.

The laughter startled me. Wild and maniacal and unlike any sound I'd ever heard from my father. For a moment my mind couldn't process it, couldn't understand it. But then reality hit like a load of bricks crashing over me.

He was laughing at me.

He was amused by my misery.

And I had no one to blame but myself.

His figure faded then, and the last image I saw was of his delight at my self-destruction.

The tears came then, and because I could not hold back any longer, I let them. I cried. And cried. And cried.

Adrian strolled into the girls' bathroom like it was no big deal, and sat down beside me. I lifted my eyes to his, positive that I looked like a red raccoon. He said nothing. Just reached for me and pulled me into his lap.

As his arms came around me I remembered the conversation I wanted to have with him, but now was not the time. I was devastated and he was here, not saying a word, not trying to fix things, not giving me unwanted advice. Just holding me, letting his warmth seep into me as the last few tears slid down my cheeks.

His ability to comfort me was almost supernatural, and I wondered again about the visions I'd seen of him in my room. Whoever or whatever he was, I needed him.

I'd figure out the rest later.

CHAPTER 14

Adrian walked me to the front office and told the secretary I wasn't feeling well. Understatement of the year. She promptly called my mom to come and pick me up.

As I took a seat in the waiting area, I realized I hadn't said the first word to Adrian since he waltzed into the girls' restroom.

"Thanks," I whispered, fixing my eyes on the speckled white tiles of the floor.

"Of course." He sat next to me and leaned close, propping his elbows in his knees. "I'll bring your assignments over after school and make sure you get caught up on Pre-Cal."

I nodded. Where was the sense of comfort he usually gave me? Why was my gut still churning inside? Maybe Adrian didn't have superpowers after all.

I shook my head at my own foolishness. Thinking Adrian had some kind of supernatural ability. Geez.

"It's okay to feel what you're feeling," he said. "Sometimes you've got to feel the hurt, go through it, before you can start to heal."

I looked at him then, turned his words of wisdom over in my head. I wasn't sure about healing, but I was sure as hell feeling the hurt.

After the initial check of my forehead for fever and the typical questions about nausea, headache, and sore throat – of which nausea was the only thing I admitted to – my mom drove me home. We didn't talk.

A hundred different emotions ran through me. Anger. Bitterness. Humiliation. Fear. Confusion. And the ever-present grief and guilt. It all bubbled and simmered like a pool of poison ready to erupt.

Just as mom turned into the driveway, I broke the silence.

"Did you know the woman Dad cheated with?"

Mom looked at me, and I pinned her with my gaze, wanting to know I was dead serious. I saw the reluctance in her eyes. She did not want to go there. I also knew the moment she decided to answer me, because her expression changed, like she knew if I was giving her an opening to talk about Dad, she'd better take it.

"I knew her name, but not much else," she said, pulling the car to a stop in the driveway. "He said she'd moved to town a few years ago and wasn't connected to anyone here."

True enough. I remembered when Courtney came to Rison Middle School in the seventh grade.

"What was her name?"

"Zoe, don't do this," Mom pleaded. "Don't dredge up specifics. It won't change what happened."

"What was her name, Mom?" I demanded.

She took a deep breath and shook her head. "Mitzi Wayne."

Bingo.

"That's Courtney Powell's mother."

"Oh God." Mom's voice shook. "The different last names. I never put it together."

"Yeah, well Courtney did. She dropped it on me in the lobby in front of everyone."

I watched my mom's heart break all over again, as pain filled her eyes. "Zoe…"

"Don't say you're sorry," I said, opening the car door and grabbing my backpack. "He's the one who did it. Just don't expect me to get over it any time soon."

"I'll call the office," she said just before I got out of the car. Desperation laced her voice. "I'll tell them I can't come back in today."

"Go back to the office, Mom." I stepped out of the car, but turned back to face her. "I don't want company. And if you stay, I'm not talking to you about this."

I shut the car door with a quiet click rather than a slam, then marched to the house, went inside, and cried all over again.

I heard the roar of Adrian's motorcycle pulling into the driveway. Glancing at the clock, I knew he had come straight here from school.

I made my way to the front door and stepped out onto the porch, trying without much success to tamp down on the mountain of self-pity I'd wallowed in all day.

He cut the engine and parked the bike, placing his helmet on the seat and unhooking his book bag from the back where it was secured with the bungee cord.

"Have you been alone all day?" he asked, approaching the front porch.

I nodded, and I could tell that my confirmation did not sit well with him.

"Did you tell your mom?" He stopped at the edge of the sidewalk, not stepping up onto the porch, putting us at eye-level.

"Yes," I said. "She tried to insist on staying home the rest of the day, but I told her I didn't want company."

"That still true?" he asked with an almost-grin and questioning eyes. "Do you still not want company?"

"I always want your company," I whispered, mustering what I could of a smile. "Come on in."

His eyes narrowed. "Your mom going to be okay with that?"

I shrugged. At this point, I didn't care whether she was or not. But, I wanted Adrian's first impression on Mom to be a good one. "As long as she finds us fully clothed somewhere other than the bedroom, it'll be fine."

He stepped up onto the porch, snaking an arm around my waist and pulling me close enough to press a brief kiss to my forehead. "The kitchen table it is then."

And despite everything that had happened, my insides swooned.

Homework took a bit longer than usual, because I had to catch up on everything, but Adrian and I managed to work through it all and get Pre-Calculus finished just as Mom came in the door. Adrian's normally calm expression tensed up, nervousness showing in his eyes.

"You wanted to meet my mom," I said, nudging him with my elbow.

"Zoe?" Mom called from the living room.

"Kitchen," I replied.

"Zoe, we're going to have to –" She stopped mid-sentence, stepping into the kitchen and finding Adrian with me.

"Mom, this is Adrian Shaw, Ms. Turner's nephew. He came by to bring my assignments to me."

"Oh." She dropped her keys on the counter, the metal clanking together as she sat her purse beside them. "That was very nice of you."

"Nice to meet you Mrs. Gray." Adrian stood, shaking my mom's hand like a perfect gentleman. The look on her face told me she was impressed.

"Zoe told me you've been helping her with Pre-Calculus."

Adrian nodded. "Yes, ma'am."

"He's a math genius, Mom," I said, startled by the chipper ring to my voice. But then again, Adrian tended to bring that out in me.

Mom's eyes cut toward me, surprise on her face. I knew she still wanted to talk about the big who-my-dad-banged-on-the-side revelation, but she must've decided it could wait. Thank God.

"Adrian, can you stay for dinner?" Mom asked, heading for the refrigerator.

Adrian looked at me, gauging my reaction to the invitation. If it would put off the inevitable share-your-feelings session with my mom, I was all for it. Besides, I liked having him around.

I just smiled and shrugged my shoulders.

"Thanks Mrs. Gray. That would be great."

After dinner, we ended up back at the creek bank. Adrian's impeccable manners and genuine demeanor had won Mom over enough that she didn't object, despite that fact that I still didn't exactly have social privileges.

We didn't talk as we spread the blanket he'd pulled from the saddlebag out on the grass, directly beneath a huge oak tree that was probably older than the town.

The worn, rust-colored wool was soft against my legs as we sat. Adrian leaned against the tree trunk, and I leaned against Adrian with his arm around me. The water in the creek trickled sparsely. I imagined once the semi-drought we'd been experiencing ended, the rush of water would be brisk.

Adrian turned his face toward my ear and I felt the warm rush of his breath as he whispered, "Wanna talk?"

Laying my head on his shoulder, I was silent for a long moment. Long enough that he must've thought I didn't want to talk.

"It's okay if you don't want to."

"I just don't know what to say," I said, searching for words to convey my feelings and coming up rather empty. "It's so surreal, you know? That scene in the lobby this morning, it was like adding insult to injury."

"It was lousy, that's for sure." His arm tightened around my side, and for the first time since the explosion about Courtney's mom, I felt not only the companionship of Adrian's presence, but also the warmth and soothing comfort I'd come to associate with him. "I wish I'd been there."

"I don't know why it makes a difference. I knew my dad cheated. Knowing who he cheated with shouldn't make it any worse."

"But it does."

And there was the precise reason I'd bonded so intensely with Adrian. He just *got it*. Somehow, some way, he understood.

"Yeah."

"Have you thought about..." he started to say. "Never mind."

I sat up straighter, turning to look at him, his lids lowered over baby blues full of genuine sweetness.

"What?"

"I don't want to overstep." He reached up, running his hand through a blond lock of my hair.

"You're allowed to overstep."

He let out a heavy breath, laying his hand gently against my cheek. "Have you thought about forgiving your dad?"

My eyes dropped to the blanket, the shame I felt preventing me from looking him in the eye.

Thought about it? I'd dreamed about it. And in every scenario I'd played in my mind, the result was always the same. It was too little, too late, and my hatred and contempt was the last thing he felt from me before he died.

I had no one to blame for that but myself.

And this latest shocker – that it was Courtney's mom he'd gotten busy with – had just dropped me right back in the middle of all that contempt.

"I don't know if I can," I said, more ashamed than I'd ever been in my life.

It was the truth, and I hated myself for it.

"You've got every right to feel that way." He lifted my face with a soft finger beneath my chin. "What he did was wrong on so many levels. But forgiveness isn't something you do only for the other person. It's something you do for yourself, so that you can go on with your life."

He was right. I knew he was right, and yet...

"I know that up here." I tapped my index finger against my temple. "It's all very logical. But in here," I said, placing my hand over my heart, "all I feel is this awful betrayal."

"And there's nothing wrong with you for feeling that way. What happened wasn't fair. Courtney humiliating you the way she did wasn't fair. Coming to terms with what happened to your family isn't something you're going to do on anyone else's timetable. Situations like this don't come with a manual. You'll deal with it in your own time."

His words were exactly what I needed to hear, but his pleading eyes were telling a different story.

"Why do I hear a *but* at the end of that statement?"

He reached for both of my hands, encased them with his own, and held them between us. "I want you to be able to have the life that you deserve. And the way you feel right now is hindering that."

Not exactly breaking news, I thought.

"And I'm not saying it's your fault, because it isn't. But until you can forgive, the emotional fallout from this tragedy is going to get in the way of everything. College. Your future plans. Your relationship with your mom. Your friendships." He picked up our joined hands and kissed my fingertips, once, twice, three times. "*This*." His eyes locked on mine. "You and me."

Fear shot through me, hot and sharp, lancing nerves that were already raw and exposed. Was he saying he couldn't handle being with such a basket case? Not that I'd fault him for that, but the idea of losing him filled me with panic.

"I don't blame you if you don't want to stick around." My voice quivered, threatening to give away the dread inside me.

"I'm not trying to rush or push you, or tell you just to get over it. I know it's not that simple," he said, squeezing my hands. "And I don't want to go any-where."

I stared back down at the blanket.

"Look at me Zoe."

When I looked up at him, he leaned close, until we were practically nose-to-nose. "I don't want to go anywhere. I want to stay here with you. But…" He stopped, took a deep breath as if he was trying to find the right words. "Sometimes things happen and we don't get what we want. Especially at our age. Sometimes things are out of our control."

He was being awfully cryptic, but I think I got the point. "Are you afraid your parents will insist you go to Europe to be with them?"

"Something like that isn't outside the realm of possibility," he said. "And if that happens, if I have to leave, I want things solid between us. I don't want to have to leave until you and I are, well… until we're are a unit."

I liked that idea, the two of us as a unit. I also knew he was right. About all of it. I just didn't know how to make it happen.

"I'll try," I said. "I'll work really hard on the forgiveness thing."

His face lit up, hope and happiness evident in his smile. "I'll help."

"You already have."

I meant what I'd said about trying. But not even the look in his eyes could kill the doubt in my soul. Somewhere deep in my heart was the firm belief that I would live with this misery for the rest of my life.

And that I absolutely, positively deserved it.

CHAPTER 15

Awful didn't even begin to describe the next morning at school. The bright-white walls of the new school felt like a prison, plain and colorless, confining me to the humiliation I'd suffered here the previous day. When I wasn't fielding questions about the validity of Courtney's claims, I was enduring looks of the poor-pitiful-Zoe variety from every direction.

I lost count of how many times I said, "My parents' marriage was their business before my dad died, and it's still their business", or something to that effect. I felt like I was at a never ending press conference and all I could say was "no comment".

For the most part, I said nothing else. Until I encountered Viv and Daniel at my locker.

"Is it true?" Daniel spoke while Viv looked at the floor. "Or was she just being a bitch?"

Since they'd witnessed the messy exchange yesterday, I felt like I owed them the truth. Then there was the fact that my father's infidelity was the part of the story I'd withheld from Viv, and I figured it was time to come clean.

"She was definitely being a bitch," I began. "But what she said was true."

"And you didn't know?" Daniel asked.

Viv looked up at me then, all kinds of confusion swimming in her eyes. Compassion and regret, and at the same time distrust and uncertainty. In that moment I wished so badly that I'd told her everything. She would've been there for me, no questions asked.

Hindsight.

"I knew about the affair," I admitted and watched Viv's eyes turn misty and sad. "Just not who it was with."

The hurt in Viv's eyes cut me to my soul. I knew she thought I hadn't trusted her enough to confide in her and I searched every corner of my brain for words to express that it had nothing to do with not trusting her and everything to do with how ashamed I was of the situation.

Still she said nothing. She just looked away.

"Well, that really sucks," Daniel said. "And Courtney totally sucks for telling you that way."

"Viv, I just wanted to forget it," I whispered, stepping around to stand directly in front of her.

"You could've told me," she replied, eyes still glued to the beige tile floor. "I'd have listened."

"I know. I was just so embarrassed. I didn't talk about it with anyone, not even Mom, until Adrian."

Her eyes shot to mine, narrowing in disbelief. "You told Adrian?"

And yeah. That had not been the best thing to say.

Daniel had the good sense to slip away.

"Telling him just sort of happened the other night. Mom and I almost had a fight and I went for a walk. I ran into him and just sort of unloaded."

"I'm your best friend," she said, her voice an eerie, startling kind of calm. "Or at least I thought I was. You spent the whole summer with those two skanks, and now that you've detached yourself from them, you turn to Adrian instead of me?"

"It's not him *instead* of you. It's just…"

"Forget it." She interrupted me. "You're hurting and I know that. I'm really sorry about that. But I can't take being dropped by you again."

And then she turned and walked away.

My heart constricted until I was sure my blood could no longer be circulating. What had I done? In my grief-wallowing selfishness had I killed the friendship that mattered most?

"She'll be okay." Adrian's voice came from over my shoulder.

He told me last night that I had to forgive and move on before the other parts of my life would thrive again. But after the carnage of my dad's stupidity was finished wrecking my existence, what would be left?

"And you want me to forgive him?" I asked, not looking back at him. I laughed, but out of irony not humor. "He couldn't keep his pants on, and the fallout from it is destroying my life. His no-conscience dick has now cost me my best friend."

"You forgive for yourself, for your own well-being." He took me by the shoulders and turned me to face him. "Love can't grow where bitterness takes root."

"Thanks for the philosophy lesson, but so far love hasn't done a damn bit of good."

I left him standing in the hall and didn't look back as I headed for my homeroom.

The nasty way I'd spoken to Adrian was just one more thing to add to my list of reasons to hate myself. He hadn't deserved that venom. He'd done nothing but be kind and understanding, and he'd listened without giving unsolicited advice when all my mom wanted to do was talk it out.

Even as I beat myself up over it in Pre-Calculus, I knew he wouldn't act any different toward me the next time I saw him. He wouldn't hold it against me. He'd just go on being exactly the same thoughtful, considerate guy he'd always been.

As Mrs. Faulkner droned on and on about polynomial equations – whatever the heck that was – sounding like about as enthusiastic as a pile of rocks, I replayed our conversation from the night before.

It would be better for Adrian if the two of us just cut our losses now. I would just go on dragging him down, and he totally didn't deserve the crazy that came standard with me these days.

I jotted down the homework assignment and allowed myself a moment to wonder how in the world I'd get through this class without Adrian's help, before deciding it didn't really make any difference. Who cared if I flunked Pre-Cal? It wasn't like I was ever going to be a physicist or math professor. I'd be doing good to just get back to normal again, though I'd begun to think this *was* my new normal.

Besides, I might as well get used to being without Adrian. If I didn't end it now, he'd walk away eventually anyway. And why not? I'd lost my dad. I'd lost Vivian. Seemed it was only a matter of time before everyone important was gone. I could at least make sure some of it was on my own terms.

Life sucked.

CHAPTER 16

I strategically avoided Adrian – and most everyone else – all morning long. Thanks to the unpleasant conversation with Viv, and my subsequent spitefulness to Adrian, I hadn't stopped at my locker before homeroom to leave my backpack. Instead, I just drug it with me. When the bell rang to end each class, I'd pretend to look through it for some unnamed object necessary for the next class, giving the halls a chance to clear before I ventured out.

Several times, I hid in the bathroom until I could move to my next class without interacting with anyone.

Then I made the unfortunate decision to drop the backpack at my locker before going to the cafeteria. And got caught in the pre-lunch melee.

Scads of kids crowded the hall, all pushing through to their lockers, hoping to beat the second wave of lunchers to the line.

As if school lunch was something to get that excited about.

Darting my eyes back and forth, I scanned the crowd for Adrian, Viv, Courtney, or Nikki, and breathed a sigh of relief when I saw none of them.

How sad that I now thought of Adrian and Viv in the same context as Nikki and Courtney.

I grabbed onto the built-in combination lock, hurrying to open my locker and be done with it. It's true what they say about haste making waste, because I misdialed the combination three times.

Giving Courtney just the opportunity she needed.

"Zoe." Her snarky voice floated through the air like nails on a chalkboard as she leaned a shoulder against the locker next to mine. "I hated that we didn't get to finish our talk yesterday."

"We finished," I said, making my tone flat and dry in an effort to put a stop to whatever she had planned.

It was interesting to see this side of Courtney. Normally she just trailed along behind Nikki, adding *yeah* or a *that's right* to whatever dribble Nikki spit out. What had caused this change in initiative? And did it really matter?

I decided it did not.

"I have nothing to say to you." I gave up on the lock, hitching my backpack further onto my shoulder and making the decision to spend my lunch break hiding in the bathroom. Again.

"No sense denying it," she said with a roll of her eyes, as if we were talking about something as senseless as a piece of gossip. "Your dad and my mom hooked up."

I looked down the hallway, toward the lobby and the cafeteria entrance, hoping the hall had cleared enough for a quick getaway.

No luck.

Adrian stood in the lobby, looking at me with concern. Probably waiting for me, since we usually saw each other for a few minutes at lunch. No thank you. Not today.

I looked back at Courtney. "I'm not denying anything. But I won't air my family's business out in public."

Glancing back toward the lobby, Adrian still stood, but was no longer looking at me. Instead, his eyes were fixed beyond me, somewhere down the hall. I turned to try and see, but Courtney leaned closer and blocked my view.

"It's my family's business too."

"Oh please," I sneered, tired of this insanity. "If you call your mom getting it on with a married man *family business*, then you're a bigger tramp than I thought. All you've done with this latest episode is make yourself look even trashier."

Whatever she said next got lost in the roar of my pulse in my ears, as I turned away and walked toward my hiding place in the girls' restroom.

CHAPTER 17

"Zoe Gray, report to the principal's office."

The words boomed over the intercom, obnoxiously loud in the empty bathroom. Had one of the girls who'd been in and out of here reported me to the office for skipping lunch?

And was skipping lunch even considered a broken rule?

At least the halls were clear and the air fresher when I stepped out into the hall, taking a quick left and heading toward the front lobby. Maybe if I was lucky I could stretch this office visit out until after the next class change and steer clear of anyone I didn't want to talk to.

The waiting room outside Principal Burton's office reminded me of the dentist's sitting area. The maroon chairs were upholstered with some kind of heavy fabric that looked more concerned with withstanding a nuclear blast than being soft or comfortable, and the walls were lined with encouraging posters, proclaiming *Attitude is Everything* and *Education is What You Make it, So Make it Great.*

I plopped into one of the lovely chairs and noticed Mr. Austin speaking with Mr. Burton in the other room.

My visit here must have something to do with student government elections.

But when Mr. Austin looked my direction, his expression was somber. He looked back at Principal Burton and shook his head, as if he was declining something.

As he left the office, he didn't speak. My stomach sank.

Mr. Burton stepped into the lobby. "Miss Gray, come in."

Worry bubbled in my chest as heat crept into my cheeks. Somehow I knew I was walking into a trap.

"Take a seat," Mr. Burton said, pushing the door closed behind him.

I did as I was told, silently praying as he returned to his office chair on the other side of the desk. The ominous vibe in the room made the air heavy and difficult to breathe.

"We found the items that were taken from Mr. Austin's classroom." Mr. Burton rested his elbows on the desk, leaning across just enough that I could see disappointment dripping from his expression. And smell the old man aftershave he must've used copious amounts of.

"I don't know what you're talking about," I said, sitting up a little straighter. "I haven't even been to Mr. Austin's class yet."

"We found his iPhone and digital camera in your locker."

A meteor landing directly on my head couldn't have stunned me more. My chest pounded as if I'd run a marathon, panic racing through my veins.

"I didn't steal them." The quick denial sounded pitiful, but it was all I could come up with. "I swear I didn't."

"He reported the items missing at the beginning of fifth period," Mr. Burton explained. "Security video has shown you making a point to only be in the hallway after it's cleared, as if you didn't want to be seen. Further, it shows you stopping at your locker between fourth and fifth period, then making your way to the girls' restroom where it appears you stayed."

Are you freaking kidding me? All I'd wanted was to avoid having to talk to people. I couldn't believe my attempt at a low profile had put me in the interrogation room.

"The video footage is suspicious enough, but finding the items in your locker is the most damaging piece of evidence."

"I haven't been in Mr. Austin's room. Check your video again. You won't see me going into his room."

"The time lapse between camera shots is enough that you could've gone in, taken the items from his desk, and been gone before the camera outside his room picked up again."

And now I was pissed. The stupid security video was enough to make me look suspicious, but faulty enough not to prove me innocent. "Sounds like the security video doesn't do a lot of good."

I knew it came across as smart-ass, but I didn't care. I was as good as guilty in his book anyway.

"That tone isn't helping," Mr. Burton scolded.

No kidding.

What was worse was the fact that Mr. Austin thought I'd stolen from him. First of all, I was not a thief. Second of all, even if I was, Mr. Austin was the last person I'd steal from. I'm sure my run for student government was dead in the water now.

Not that I really cared. But yeah… I did care. I'd just begun to try and reclaim a little of my life, agreeing to run for class secretary, and now that was over before it even got started.

"Your mother has already been called."

Fan-freaking-tastic. I'd never see my car keys again.

"She's on her way to get you," he said. "You're suspended for three days."

"Suspended?" I'd never even been to the principal's office for discipline before.

"Be glad that's all it is." Mr. Burton pushed back from his desk. "Mr. Austin could've pressed charges, but chose not to."

My heart sank. Just the thought of my favorite teacher even having to consider taking legal action against me made me sick to my stomach.

And then Mom walked in the door.

CHAPTER 18

"You are not to leave this house." Mom's tone was matter-of-fact as she grabbed her purse and began digging for her keys. "For any reason."

We'd been all through this when she picked me up from school yesterday afternoon, but I figured it must've made her feel better to hash it all out again.

All sorts of retorts bounced around in my mind. *What if the house is on fire? Can I leave then? What if someone breaks in and attacks me? Am I allowed to run away from him?*

I thought better of it and kept them all to myself.

"Fine." I did my best to make my voice void of emotion.

"Tomorrow I'll be home with you all day, but I couldn't make arrangements to be off on such short notice today."

And of course, the fact that she would have to take an unpaid day from work tomorrow was completely my fault.

I said nothing. Just sat at the kitchen table staring at my bare feet.

"I will call every hour," she went on. "On the land-line. Your cell phone is in my purse, along with the car keys I've been keeping for weeks. And I will be back on my lunch hour."

Whatever.

"And at some point, whether you want to or not, you are going to talk to me about this. You don't get to hide behind your walls for months on end this time."

"I told you the truth yesterday." I whispered, because it was the only way to keep the hurt from showing in my voice. I didn't want her to know how devastated I'd been when she didn't believe me.

"I'd like to believe you, but you've made that next to impossible."

Right. And now would not be the best time to point out that she'd either forgotten or failed to notice that I really had been starting to come out of my funk.

Didn't matter anyway. I was right back in the funk thanks to this latest drama.

"I have to leave for work now," she said. "Do some thinking today. And maybe think about someone other than yourself." And then she was gone.

For the briefest of moments I thought with longing about the first time I'd gone out drinking with Nikki and Courtney. Not that I missed the two of them. I certainly did not. But I couldn't help but remember that first hit of alcohol. The burning sensation that I felt all the way down my chest. The way my limbs had begun to feel rubbery and loose. The way that all at once nothing hurt anymore. Memories didn't stab at me like a dagger.

A shame that the means to such a blissful end had to be so dangerous. And illegal.

But no. I would not fall back into that trap. I might be miserable and lonely and all sorts of other unpleasant things for the rest of my life, but I would not be a drunk.

I at least had a choice in that.

Pushing up from the kitchen table, I grabbed a back of nacho chips and headed for the couch.

The rest of my morning consisted of meaningless reruns and junk food. Anything to keep my mind occupied with drivel rather than the mess that was my life. When thoughts of Adrian, Vivian, and my dad threatened to creep in, I slammed them back with chocolate or chips or loud music.

Mom's suggestion that I spend the day in reflection was about as effective as trying to dry up a river with a cotton swab. I could reflect all day on Mr. Austin's stolen items and I still wouldn't be guilty of stealing them.

However, I was guilty of plenty, and that's what coursed through my brain during my hours of thinking of someone other than myself. Namely, all the people I've hurt or pushed away.

I hid the junk food when Mom came home for lunch and pulled out a book assigned by my English teacher. She offered me lunch, in a much nicer voice than the one she berated me with this morning, but I refused and told her I wasn't hungry. She thought I was being pouty, which was partially true, but she didn't know about the candy and nacho chips.

The afternoon was more junk food and music, but I did manage a nap for no other reason than sheer boredom. I waffled back and forth between wishing the time would pass faster and dreading the moment Mom came home. Finally, I popped open my laptop and checked my email, for lack of anything better to do.

And found a new message from Lea.

Hello Zoe. I know the start of the school year must be busy. You must be so excited to start your senior year. I'm sure there are dances and ballgames and all sorts of fun things! I just wanted you to know that I'm thinking of you and looking forward to hearing from you again. Our new computers and improved technology at the center have made it much easier to access email and the internet. I'll be able to respond more quickly to you now. And if you don't mind, keep a little girl named Ruby in your prayers. She is a regular here at the center. A sweet and vibrant girl. She has pneumonia and is really suffering. We are all anxious for her to recover and get her strength back. Take care and enjoy your senior year! Love, Lea.

Again, I closed the email without replying. My problems seemed so small in comparison to what Lea just described. And even though I knew in my head that wallowing in this misery was stupid and detrimental, I didn't have the power to stop it. Lea didn't deserve to have all of my issues dumped on her when she had so much else to focus on.

When I heard Mom's keys in the door, an hour earlier than usual, I closed my laptop and pretended to still be sleeping. Her footsteps stopped as she came through the living room and I could tell she was looking at me lying on the couch.

She headed to the kitchen and had just set her keys on the counter when the phone rang.

From her end of the conversation, I could tell it was Mr. Burton. I sat up and rolled my eyes, quite sure he was delivering more great news. I picked up my book and tuned them out.

Mom lowered her voice. Even though I couldn't understand her, the frustration in her tone was evident.

Great.

"That was Principal Burton," Mom said, coming into the living room a few minutes later.

I gave a noncommittal grunt.

"Another student has a video," she began, dropping to sit next to me on the sofa. "It's a cell phone video of the hallway when Mr. Austin's things were stolen. The student didn't realize until today that he'd inadvertently taped someone putting the items in your locker. He showed it to Mr. Burton."

It took a second for her words to sink in. When they did it was with a thud in the bottom of my stomach, a weird combination of relief and uncertainty. "So I've been cleared?"

She nodded. "The administration met together after school. Your punishment has been revoked, of course." She sat down next to me. "Zoe, I'm so sorry. I wanted to believe you. I just didn't know what to think."

"Save it Mom." I shook my head to stop her from continuing. "I know I've been a real pill for a while, but I was making an effort. It would've been nice to have the benefit of the doubt from someone."

Thankfully, she didn't respond. There was just no way I could have a conversation with her right now. My brain was still processing the fact that I was off the hook, and wondering who in the world had managed to get a cell phone video. True, the hall had been crowded, but most kids had been barreling toward the cafeteria. Of course, I'd been busy dealing with Courtney and her unceremonious stop at my locker, so it's not like I would've noticed.

But I had noticed Adrian at the end of the hallway.

Adrian.

And just like that I knew what I needed to do.

"Mom, can I please have my car keys?" I figured she might feel bad enough about not believing me that she'd hand them over, at least temporarily. "Just for tonight. I'll give them back. I just need to clear my head."

I could tell she struggled with the idea, but even she had to admit that this latest blunder had not been mine.

Without a word, she walked to the kitchen, returning seconds later with my keys. And my cell phone.

"I ate junk food all day, so I'm not hungry. But I won't be out late. I promise." I thought it would be a good idea to play nice.

She took a deep breath. "Okay."

I headed for the door.

My hand was on the doorknob when her voice stopped me.

"Zoe," she said, and I paused and turned around. "I love you. I realize it's been far too long since I said that."

Emotion clogged my throat, and though I'd spent the better part of the day completely pissed at her for doubting me, I couldn't help but smile.

CHAPTER 19

Adrian's bike stood, gleaming black in the late afternoon sun, pulled to the gravel shoulder near the creek. I managed to park my car and turn off the ignition, though in my haze of urgency I didn't remember either.

When I hit the clearing he was there. I wasn't surprised. Nothing about him surprised me anymore.

The wind moved quietly around me, lifting my hair from my shoulders, comforting and peaceful. Even then I knew the feelings weren't just from the pleasant breeze.

The blanket was already spread beneath the tree, two Twix candy bars and two cans of ginger ale in the middle of it. The sight of the chocolate might've been enough to make me groan after all I'd eaten during the day, were it not for the obvious fact.

He was waiting for me.

If I'd needed another bit of confirmation that Adrian was more than met the eye, finding him here was it.

"You knew I'd come here." It wasn't a question.

"I had a hunch." He shrugged his shoulders and leaned his head toward the blanket. "Come sit?"

It seemed as good a place as any to have this conversation, so I walked over and sat, not next to him this time, but across. A large part of me wanted to snuggle up beside him, the same way I had the last time we sat here, but I reminded myself I'd decided alone was the best way to go.

And there was the matter of all the questions I had.

"Mr. Burton called earlier," I said, reaching for a ginger ale. The top popped with a satisfying fizz. "Told my mom about the video."

He just nodded, opening his own drink.

"I know it was you."

He smiled, lifting a shoulder in nonchalance.

"First of all, thank you," I whispered.

"You're welcome."

"Second of all, there's no way you could've made that video." I looked directly at him, searching his eyes for any hint of explanation. "You weren't at that end of the hall. You were in the lobby. I saw you."

He didn't say anything, just looked at me with raised eyebrows.

"Did someone else video it and give it to you."

He shook his head. "I did it."

"How?" I breathed, my voice barely above a whisper. Sitting my drink to the side, I scooted closer, the fabric of the blanket soft beneath my legs. He hadn't denied being in the lobby, but he insisted he'd been the one to shoot the cell phone video.

"How do you think I did it?" He scooted closer too and leaned down so we were eye to eye.

And here it was. The moment of truth.

"I think you're something other than human." The words left my mouth in one big rush, like if I'd hesitated in the least they would never have been voiced. I could not believe I'd just said that out loud. But how else could I describe all the things that were unexplained about Adrian and his presence in my life?

He said nothing, but the slight smile on his face and the light in his eyes told me to keep going. Naturally, he would make me pick every last detail out of him.

"The morning after the car wreck," I whispered, halfway afraid of what his answer would be. "Were you in my bedroom, sitting on my bean bag?"

"Yes." His answer was simple and swift.

Holy cow. Even though I'd *known*, shock zinged through me at his affirmation.

"The night I dreamed about seeing my dad at the cemetery?"

"I was there that night too. And yesterday, when you saw your dad in the bathroom at school."

I couldn't keep up with the spinning in my mind. How could he have known about either of those things?

Remembering the night of the car accident and those arms around me, I asked, "After the car wreck, did you get me out of the car?"

He smiled, nodded. "Yes. I took you home."

"What are you, Adrian?" My mind spun with possibilities. The more questions he answered the more I wanted to ask, and yet it seemed so silly to put words to my suspicions. I dropped my eyes to the blanket. "Some kind of superhero? An angel?"

"Not really an angel, but there are some similarities. Angels are supernatural beings. I'm human. Just like you, but with a few... extras."

"That doesn't really tell me what you are." The creek trickled softly in the background, its timbre calm and serene, and I smiled despite the crazy nature of this conversation.

"We're called *Messengers*."

"We?" Of course there would be more.

He nodded. "It's not really an official title, but I guess over the years that's just how we've come to think of ourselves. The best way to describe it is that we're a sub-species of humans. We were created to *assist* in certain situations."

Assist. Sounded like a basketball play, instead of something so huge it re-shaped your reality.

"Are you immortal?" I could not believe that just came out of my mouth.

He shook his head.

"But you have *extras*?"

"Yes."

"When I saw you in my bedroom – both times – you were there one minute, then I blinked and you were gone. Can you make yourself invisible?"

He nodded, and my reality shifted even more. A wicked little smile tugged at his lips, like he was enjoying watching me figure it all out.

"My Pre-Cal book? The first day we met. Did you do that?"

"Yes."

His one-word answers, while truthful, were becoming annoying. "What, you used your superpowers of invisibility to return the book to my locker?"

Adrian promptly cracked up. "When you put it like that it sounds like something out of a comic book," he said between bursts of laughter. "But yeah, something like that."

"Can you fly faster than a speeding bullet?" I asked. "Is that how you got the book from my house and put it back in my locker?"

"No." He shook his head. "We don't fly. But..."

He paused for dramatic effect, and it worked. I felt like a kid being told a bedtime story, waiting to see what happened next.

"What?"

He opened his candy bar, offering one of the pieces to me, and said, "We can teleport."

"No way!"

Holy freaking cow! My mind spun like a tilt-a-whirl at the county fair.

"Not with any loud noise or huge gust of wind or anything you might see in a sci-fi movie. It's more like we just will ourselves to a different place. Comes in handy when we're on assignment."

"Assignment?"

"The Boss," he said, pointing his index finger up toward the sky, "assigns us to certain people or situations, to help things work out in the best possible way."

And just like that, the wonder of all that Adrian was became a weight in the center of my chest as I realized the *why* of his presence in my life.

"I'm your assignment."

There was some comfort in the fact that the *Boss*, as Adrian referred to Him, had taken such an interest in my situation, but knowing that I was an *assignment* to Adrian cut deep.

"Yes," he said, tentatively reaching for one of my hands. When I didn't pull away, he grasped my fingers and continued. "But not *just* an assignment."

"I bet you say that to all the girls." Cliché, I knew, but it was the best I could do to make light in this situation that, despite my efforts to push him away, was breaking my heart.

I didn't want to be his assignment.

"Zoe, do you remember when I told you that I was happy?"

I nodded. I'd never forget that moment. Ever.

"Do you remember that I said I didn't expect to be happy? That I thought coming here was just something else I had to do?"

"I remember."

"I meant that," he said, squeezing my hand again. "I'm happy. With you."

I didn't even remember what happiness felt like anymore, but I figured what I felt with Adrian was something pretty close. But there was still the matter of the huge mess my life was in, the fact that I had yet to truly forgive my father, and the many, many questions I still had for Adrian.

Since I could do nothing about the mess or forgiveness at the moment, I decided to keep going with the questions.

"Why did you rescue me from the car wreck," I asked. "Why not just let me get arrested with Nikki and Courtney and learn my lesson the hard way."

"I think you did learn your lesson the hard way," he said. "If you'd gone to jail with them, it would've only tied you to them even deeper. You'd have had a common problem, a common goal, and what you needed was a reason to leave them in the dust."

"It worked," I admitted.

Dusk began to settle around us, cloaking the clearing with the shadows of the trees that surrounded us. Through the trees the sky began to blush an opaque pink color as the sun started its descent. I had always loved dusk. I'd always thought of it as the time of day when heaven was closest to earth, when the sun met the horizon and the sky glowed with color.

I couldn't help but think it fitting to be here with Adrian, at this precise moment.

"I've never told anyone what I am." He shifted the conversation, as if somehow sensing the overwhelming feelings bubbling inside of me. "Neither has my dad. Well, except for my mom. I never imagined telling anyone the truth about myself, so this is uncharted territory for me."

"Are you not supposed to tell anyone?" I asked, worried that he might get into some kind of trouble for telling me.

"There's not like a vow of secrecy or anything, but our purpose is to help the people we're assigned to, and when we're on assignment it's easier to succeed if no one knows we're there working behind the scenes. I doubt we'd be very effective if the whole world knew we existed. I guess I'm afraid that revealing myself will compromise my assignment."

"Is there some kind of punishment if you don't succeed?"

"The Boss is pretty forgiving." He smiled, squeezing my hand. "But if I fail here, with you, I won't be able to forgive myself."

"What exactly is your assignment?"

"To help you forgive your father, and yourself." He scooted close enough that our knees touched. "So that your life can go on."

"I haven't been very accommodating, have I?" It dawned on me just how much he'd sacrificed to come here, to help a girl he'd never met. He lived a life that revolved around serving and helping other people. And so far I'd done precious little to make his job easy.

"You've made progress," he said with a smile. "This is my first solo assignment. Until now I've worked with my dad, so I've seen the whole gamut of situations."

The sun dipped lower, lighting the sky in a bright orange. The sunset reminded me that I'd promised my mom I would be home early.

"As much as I don't want to, I've got to head home before long," I said. "Mom reluctantly let me drive my car, and I know I'm still on thin ice with her, so I can't be late."

"Okay." He touched my cheek, the gesture sweet and reassuring. "I'm glad we talked. Glad you know the truth about me, awkward as it is."

"Before I go, I have to know how you made that video."

His eyes dropped, and he shoved one hand through his hair. Clearly he was uncomfortable with the subject.

"Please," I asked. "I'm really really grateful, but I need to know how you did it."

"There are other abilities," he began. "Things I haven't told you about yet."

I pressed on. "And they helped you record a video you were in no position to record how?"

"I can manipulate time. Revisit places, events."

Already on overload, my brain threatened to explode or shut down completely. "You mean time travel?" I barely choked out the words.

"Not exactly," he said. "I can't go back and be a part of a previous time. I can go back and observe, but not interact."

"So no one would be able to see you?"

"Right."

"You jumped back to that moment didn't you?" Finally the pieces began to fit. "You went back and watched Nikki steal that stuff out of Mr. Austin's room and then stow it in my locker."

"I could see you from the lobby, and I knew Courtney was at your locker. I was worried about you. I could see beyond her a bit, and it was obvious she was trying to block your view of whatever was going on. I caught a glimpse of Nikki coming out of Mr. Austin's room. I knew they were up to something but I wasn't sure what. When I heard later that you'd been suspended for stealing something from Mr. Austin, I realized what they'd done."

"And you went back to watch," I breathed, pretty much in awe of what he'd done for me. "That's when you recorded that video."

He nodded.

"Thank you," I said. "Again."

"Revisiting is not a skill we're supposed to throw around frivolously. It's only supposed to come into play when it will benefit the assignment. Using it for personal gain or for entertainment, well, it doesn't look good on the resume."

"But this wasn't for your personal gain," I said. "You didn't do it for yourself. You did it for me."

"Everything I do for you is also for myself," he replied. "Feeling the way I do about you, everything I do to help you benefits us and what's between us. I'm still trying to decide if revisiting that moment was for the good of this assignment or just because I was so pissed at the two of them for framing you."

"I think it was probably both." I reached for his hands, which were clenched into tight fists on his knees, forcing his fingers to relax as they curled around mine. "Being accused and punished for something I didn't do was going to push me over the edge. I was already totally freaked out about Courtney's mom and my dad. Then Viv got mad at me, and it was like everything was falling down on top of me. This morning I didn't care what happened. In my mind, my life was ruined. And now I have hope again."

I made sure his eyes were on mine when I finished. "Because of what you did."

I kissed him then, as much for myself and my own desires as for guaranteeing him that he'd done the right thing for the right reasons. He'd not only rescued me, he'd done it thinking there might well be consequences for his actions. He'd *risked* for me.

His hand came against my cheek, the gentleness almost breath-taking. We lingered there a moment longer, both of us reluctant to move.

When he pulled back, it was only a breath. "When you're ready, I can take you back. You can revisit moments in the past that might make a difference. Things that you didn't see when it was all going down."

"You mean see my dad again?" The thought that that was even possible made my head swim.

"When you're ready," he repeated.

My heart raced with the yearning to say *right now*. The thought of seeing my dad again, of maybe finding some sort of closure, dangled in front of me like some kind of drug that was necessary for my survival. But the sun was even lower in the sky and I knew I needed to get home.

And I knew I needed time to digest everything I'd learned tonight and all that was now possible.

Adrian was right… when I was ready.

CHAPTER 20

L ying in bed later that night, I realized I felt more at peace than I had since before my parents separated and my family imploded. The talk with Adrian had been therapeutic, not only because I finally knew the truth about him, but because I'd given voice to the fact that I had hope again.

It was like saying the words out loud had somehow made them real.

And, indeed, in the dark of my room, with moonlight peeping through the curtains, hope simmered quietly in my heart.

Peacefulness didn't exactly equate to easy slumber. So much information circled through my mind, that it was difficult to turn the thoughts off. Moment after moment passed while my brain continued to process it all.

Eventually, however, sleep came.

I drifted into the scene like a mist that rolled silently off the water. I recognized the kitchen of my house, and my parents sitting at the table together. I wasn't so much *in* the room as I was a *presence* about the room.

I remembered this day. Two weeks prior I'd come home to find my parents at the table, exactly the way they sat today. They'd asked me to sit then dropped the bomb that had shattered my life.

On *this* day, I'd come home from school, pissed to find my dad's car in the driveway. He'd been staying in Lexington with his brother, Nolan, since the day he obliterated our family, and I hadn't missed him. Hadn't I made it clear I didn't want to see him again?

Even as the thought ran through my dream, I heard the front door open, listened as angry footsteps stomped toward my bedroom.

"Zoe," my mom called. "Please come to the kitchen."

I knew this was not Adrian's doing. He hadn't taken me back to *revisit* this day. I'd experienced it the first time. This was simply a dream of remembrance.

I knew exactly what happened.

Mom called again, and I knew I had no choice.

My eyes almost rolled back into my head. Did I really have to go through this again? Hadn't we said it all the last time he was here?

I threw my backpack against my bedroom door and turned to stomp down the hall, pasting my most sullen expression on my face. If Dad wanted to talk, fine. He could talk. I wasn't saying a word.

I flopped down into a kitchen chair, folded my arms across my chest, and looked at the floor, refusing to make eye contact with either of them.

"Your dad and I have made arrangements to start counseling," Mom said. "Separately at first, but together after a while."

I continued staring at my feet, not acknowledging her at all.

"Zoe, you can't just..." Mom started to scold me, but Dad interrupted.

"Donna, it's okay," he said. "She's got every right to be angry, just like you."

I heard her take a deep breath. "Eventually we need you to be a part of our sessions. We need to work through this as a family."

I lifted one shoulder, completely non-committal.

Mom started to speak again, and I just knew if she defended him again I'd explode.

Dad talked first. "We won't force you before you're ready."

Funny that he was the parent demonstrating the most sense at this moment. Too bad he didn't have any sense when it came to keeping his pants on.

"And I know you don't want to talk to me. That's okay." He turned slightly to face me, but I didn't look at him. All I saw was the legs of the chair moving. "I sent you an email. It's not the way I want to communicate with you, but I wanted to do something to tell you how much I love you. When you're ready to talk, I'll be here, ready to listen."

Ready to listen? Well, fine then. He could listen. "Don't hold your breath waiting for me to suddenly spill my guts. But if you want to listen, listen to this." I pushed the chair back from the table and stood up, ready to make my escape once I finished. "You make me want to throw up. I can't even look at you." Bile rose up in throat, and I forced it back down. "It makes me sick that your DNA is part of me." Then I glared at him, looking him in the face for the first time. "You didn't just cheat on Mom. You cheated on me, too. And I hate you for it. I wish you were dead."

And those were the last words I ever spoke to my father.

The slam of the door as I entered my bedroom jolted me awake.

I sat straight up in the bed, taking in the darkness that told me it was still the middle of the night. I grabbed my cell from the nightstand, registering the time. Three o'clock a.m. I didn't feel Adrian's presence, but I looked at the beanbag anyway, slightly disappointed not to find him.

I knew the dream wasn't from him. Memories of my dad had been stirred up all day, especially after my time at the creek with Adrian. I figured my subconscious was trying to work something out by pulling that memory from my brain and dropping it into my dream.

But what?

I replayed the scene in my mind, from arriving home to find Dad's car in the driveway to the moment I stormed out of the kitchen. Very little had actually been said. Just Mom announcing their marital counseling. Dad telling me I had the right to be angry.

I sent you an email earlier today.

Dad's email. A sinking feeling swept through me, threatening to cause my junk food binge to make a reappearance. How could I have forgotten? I'd been so pissed off that day, I'd opened my email as soon as he'd left and stuck his message into my junk folder without reading it.

And now, four months later, it waited for me.

Could I read it now, with less hatred and bitterness? Was it possible the time that had passed had softened me toward what he had to say? Or would reading it dredge up every ounce of anger I'd felt that day?

The laptop on my dresser might as well have stood up and crooked a finger at me in a "come hither" motion. Of course I was going to read it. Hadn't I just been ecstatic at the thought of seeing my dad again when Adrian told me he could take me back? How could I not read the words he'd wanted me to see?

I retrieved my laptop and settled back against the pillows. With shaking hands, I logged into my email and found the message.

With one click, my dad's words appeared in front of me.

Zoe, I have no excuses for my behavior. I could talk all day about the reasons, but none of them are any excuse for what I did. I want you to know that this is not your mother's fault. She didn't do anything – or fail to do anything – that drove me away. I made bad choices. I'm responsible for them. But more than all of that, I want you to know that I love your mother, and I love you. I know you don't want to see me or talk to me, and as much as it hurts, I understand. But I will always love you, Zoe. No matter what. There's nothing you can say or do, no place you can go that is far enough away to make me stop loving you. Whatever happens with your mom and me, we're committed to being your parents. And being your dad means loving you more than anything. Forever.

CHAPTER 21

I didn't sleep much the rest of the night. Between small bits of slumber, I re-read Dad's email fifty times, thought back on that day, on all the ugly things I'd said, on the fact that I'd really meant them at the time. As Mom drove me to school, I wondered a million times what would've happened if I'd read his message that day. Would it have made a difference?

The only thing I'd come up with was that whatever had been said, whatever had gone unsaid, none of it really mattered now. I couldn't change the past. All I could do was work on the *now*.

And I really wanted to. I wanted to find some kind of peace, find a way to forgive, so I could move on with my life. So Adrian and I could have a future.

But as I headed into school, I couldn't help but wonder if all I deserved was to wallow in this misery for the rest of my life.

Adrian waited in the lobby, and even though I expected him, my heart still did a flip when I saw him. He was breathtakingly beautiful on the outside, and as I now knew, even more so on the inside.

And he was here for *me*.

I still found it so hard to believe that anyone – Adrian or his *Boss* – cared enough to go to all this effort for a nobody like me from small-town Kentucky.

"Morning." His deep voice soothed my nerves. "You rest at all?"

"A little," I answered. "I have something new to tell you, but not here. After school."

He nodded, reached for my hand.

His fingers closed around mine, warm and secure, and I smiled despite the fact that every eye in the lobby was now glued to the two of us. If there'd been any doubt before, Adrian's hand grasping mine told all of them that we were together. Handholding was like the universal high school signal for *we belong to each other*. And yeah, I'd be lying if I said that didn't thrill me to my toes.

I knew all the kids at school had heard about the theft of Mr. Austin's things and the fact that I'd been suspended for it. I could announce that I'd been vindicated, but what good would it do? They'd still stare. And truthfully, I didn't much care what they thought anymore.

In the entrance to the far hallway I saw Vivian, along with Brett, and my throat clogged. She made no move to speak to me, but her eyes still held all the hurt and distrust I'd seen yesterday. With a heavy sigh she turned away.

Adrian squeezed my hand and leaned down to whisper, "Give her time."

Just then Principal Burton came out of the office, Mr. Austin standing behind him. With a small motion of his hand, he invited me into the conference room, and I said a silent prayer of thanksgiving that he hadn't summoned me loud enough for everyone to hear.

"You know they've been suspended, right?" Adrian asked.

I figured as much. I also figured it wouldn't make any difference. Nikki's parents turned a blind eye to all her wrongdoings, and Courtney's mom was too caught up in her own drama to bother with her daughter.

I looked up at Adrian, about to ask him to come with me. Before I could get the words out, he said, "You got this."

Pressing a kiss against my cheek, he winked and added, "Text if you need me."

Once inside the room, Principal Burton launched into his apology.

"Zoe, I'm terribly sorry about the unfortunate way this played out. You've never been a problem student before, but I'm sure you realize how damaging the evidence was."

It wasn't much in the way of apologies, but it wasn't his opinion I was concerned about.

"I realize you were just doing your job," I said. "Mr. Austin, I'm much more worried about what you think after all this."

"I found it very difficult to believe that you would steal anything, from anyone," Mr. Austin said. "Even though everything pointed to you, still couldn't imagine a scenario where you'd take those things from me. I'm just very glad that someone had a video of what actually happened."

"Of course, I'm not at liberty to discuss the punishments of other students with you," Principal Burton inserted. "But I can tell you that the appropriate parties have been dealt with."

I nodded and turned my attention back to Mr. Austin. "I hope this doesn't change my status for student government elections."

"Of course not," he said. "And I'm very happy you finally decided to run for office."

The warning bell rang, and with as much politeness as I could muster, I excused myself from Principal Burton's presence and made my way down toward my locker.

The rest of the school day was blessedly uneventful. It helped that after the ugliness with Courtney, and the fact that I'd been framed for something I hadn't done, people pretty much left me alone. I welcomed the normal routine and even felt a bit thankful for the Pre-Calculus homework I didn't understand.

After school, Mom dropped me at home then headed back to her office. I almost asked her about having my car keys back, but decided to give it a few more days.

A slight humidity hung in the early September air, so I headed inside and grabbed two bottles of water and a package of chocolate chip cookies, looking forward to doing homework with Adrian.

Just as I stepped out the back door of the house, his motorcycle rumbled into the driveway. I wondered he why drove today, instead of walking like he usually did. I knew I had a long way to go in terms of moving on from the tragedy that had shaken my life, but for this afternoon, I planned to be a regular teenage girl, hanging out with a guy I was crazy about.

We dropped onto the bench of the picnic table as we'd done before, Pre-Cal books out and ready. Adrian straddled the bench like he always did, facing toward me.

"You said you had something to tell me," he said, grabbing a bottle and twisting the lid off.

"Later." I placed my fingers against his lips. "Let's just do homework and normal stuff first."

He grinned, circling my wrist with his large hand and holding his lips against my fingertips.

"I'm all for normal stuff," he said, pulling me toward him and sliding his lips over mine. Inside me, everything bubbled. All the unresolved feelings about my dad. Every bitter, nasty thought I'd had about Courtney and her mom. But most of all, something warm and beautiful – that had nothing whatsoever to do with my family crisis and everything to do with Adrian – swam through my veins and seemed to overshadow all the resentment and fill what had been hollow and lacking.

The kiss lingered, Adrian's hand finding its way to the back of my neck and tangling in my hair as he pressed kisses along my jaw and toward my ear.

"I love your hair," he whispered, his tongue tracing the sensitive skin behind my earlobe. "It's the color of sunshine."

"I love your, um…" I lost all train of thought as his teeth closed gently on my ear. And really, how had I planned on finishing that sentence? I love your dark hair? I love your motorcycle? Your baby blue eyes? None of it sounded nearly as romantic as his declaration.

"Hmm?" he murmured, his lips finding their way back to mine for one, last kiss. He leaned back to look at me, amusement dancing in his eyes. "You love my what?"

I was caught and I knew it. Might as well just be honest. "Everything," I answered, meaning it from the deepest part of my being.

He smiled and reached across the table for the textbook, his eyes never leaving mine. "Let's get to work."

My dad's face flashed through my mind, as clear as if I'd thought of him on purpose. Startled, I sat up straighter, eyes searching for Adrian but seeing nothing but my father.

You'll never be worthy of him.

Dad's words thundered in my head as if he'd said them with a megaphone.

"Zoe, what is it?" Adrian asked, concern and worry punctuated in each word.

The image of my dad disappeared, and Adrian's face filled my vision as he took my face in his hands.

"Talk to me," he pleaded.

"It was my dad," I whispered. "I didn't think of him or imagine him. He just popped into my head."

"What did he say?" he asked, leaning so close our foreheads touched.

I shook my head. How could I tell him what my dad had said when I knew it was the truth?

"Just playing with my fears again." I closed my eyes so maybe he wouldn't see that I'd withheld something from him. "Why is he doing this?"

"It's not him, Zoe. Maybe it's your own fears and insecurities. Maybe it's my Boss's enemy. Whatever it is, it is *not* your father."

"Your Boss's enemy?" I don't know why the thought hadn't occurred to me before. Adrian was a *Messenger*. Of course, I knew there was an enemy.

"His schemes run contrary to everything we try to accomplish. Naturally, he'd be thrilled for you to accept whatever lies you think your father has been telling you. But I repeat, that was *not* your father."

I wanted to believe him, but it was difficult to share his certainty when what my dad had said was absolutely true.

I would never be worthy of Adrian. And someday he'd figure it out.

But in the meantime, Adrian was here, and his efforts were helping. For his sake, I would continue to try.

After finishing our Pre-Cal assignment, I retrieved my laptop from my bedroom and rejoined Adrian at the picnic table.

"I had a dream last night," I said, clicking to open my email inbox. "About my dad."

"Was it a bad one?" Concern laced his voice, and I knew he was wondering why he hadn't been alerted to come keep watch, the way he'd done when I dreamed about my dad at the cemetery.

"It wasn't bad," I replied. "It wasn't really good, either. And it wasn't like the dream at the cemetery or the visions I've had of him since. It was just a replay of something that happened not long after he and mom separated. A memory I'd buried."

"Did it upset you?" He scooted closer, slipping his arm around my waist.

I shook my head, pulling up the email I'd remembered during the dream. "It reminded me of something my dad had said that day. He told me he'd emailed me. That it wasn't how he wanted to communicate with me, but he understood I didn't want to speak to him. It was his way of reaching out."

I pointed to the screen as the email loaded, and Adrian rested his chin on my shoulder and began to read.

"I was so mad at him," I whispered. "When he told me about the email, I went to my computer, dumped the message into my junk folder without reading it, and forgot about it until the dream last night."

Adrian squeezed me tighter as he finished reading. "Do his words make you feel any different?"

I shrugged, because I truly did not know. "It's what I expected. He said all the right things, all the things dads are supposed to say to reassure their kids. I think I'm probably more receptive to it now than I would've been that day."

"Then that's progress," Adrian said. "Just recognizing that you can receive his words in a more effective way now."

Nodding, I turned to face him, our faces only an inch apart. I wanted so badly to deserve him. "There's more."

"Another email?"

I shook my head. "More about that day. The things I said to him." My voice broke and I closed my eyes to hold back the tears.

"You were angry," Adrian whispered, pointing toward the email still displayed on the screen. "He knew that. Even told you he understood it."

"I told him I hated him." I dropped my head to his shoulder, so ashamed to utter the next words. "Told him I wished he was dead. Those were the last words I ever said to him."

Adrian lifted my face, his palms soft against my cheeks as he held me still and looked directly into my eyes. "You did not mean those words. I know you didn't mean them. You know you didn't mean them. And your father knew you didn't mean them."

"But how can he forgive me for saying such awful things?" Tears spilled down my cheeks and Adrian wiped them away. "How can I ever forgive myself?"

"You know your father has forgiven you," he whispered. "Without you even asking, he forgave you that day."

"I don't know how to get over it. I feel like the most awful person on the planet. Like I deserve all the bad things that have happened to me."

"You were angry, and you had a reason to be. No one argued that. Not even your father." He moved his hands from my face and encircled me in his arms, his embrace strong and sure. Tucking my head in the crook of his neck, he went on. "Anger that strong takes on a life of its own, and even though I know you couldn't help it at the time, you let it become your identity. When anger defines you, it's even harder to let go of."

My tears slowed down as his words began to sink in. He was right. "I don't want to be the angry girl anymore."

"You don't have to be," he whispered, squeezing me tighter. "You're already on your way."

"How do you know?"

"Could you have said that before school started?" he asked. "That you didn't want to be angry anymore? Because the girl I first met was holding on to that anger with both hands and enjoying it."

I shook my head. "No. I couldn't have honestly said that a few weeks ago."

"See." He pulled back enough to wink at me. "Progress."

"But I still feel angry."

"Feeling it is natural," he replied. "Wanting to keep it is dangerous. You've finally figured out the difference."

"Were you born with a counseling degree?" I joked, wiggling back enough to take in his expression.

"Just talented," he said with a grin.

"Knowing it was Courtney's mom shouldn't make it worse," I said, composed enough to sit back in my spot on the bench. "But somehow it does."

"Having it dumped on you in front of everyone didn't help."

"I believed my parents," I admitted. "That they wanted to work things out. At first I told myself they were just saying that so I'd feel better, but I really did believe them. Even before Dad died. But hearing Courtney say how in love my dad was with her mom, it makes me question."

"I don't think Courtney is a reliable source of information."

"She isn't," I agreed. "And my head knows that. It's my heart that's having trouble."

"What would put your heart at ease?" he asked, reaching out to twist a strand of my hair around his index finger.

"I think I need you to take me back." It seemed completely unreal that I was asking Adrian to take me back in time. Even more unreal that somehow it had become a part of my reality.

"What do you want to see?" he asked.

"Whatever I need to see to forgive him," I whispered. "And myself."

"Do you trust me to show you?"

"Yes." I gripped both his hands. "I trust you."

CHAPTER 22

When Mom pulled up in the driveway, Adrian and I were still at the picnic table. Not used to finding the two of us there when she got home from work, she headed toward us once she was out of the car.

"Adrian," she said. "Nice to see you again."

"You too, Mrs. Gray." He stood, offering his hand like the gentleman he was.

"Everything all right at school today?" she asked, as they shook hands.

I shrugged my shoulders. "As all right as it can be, I guess."

"Nikki and Courtney were suspended for what happened," Adrian said. "Or at least, that's the word anyway. Since they weren't at school, I figure it's true."

"I still don't understand why those two would have it out for you, Zoe. Or why Courtney would be so…" she broke off before she finished and dropped her eyes to the ground, clearly self-conscious about discussing it in front of Adrian.

But Adrian did what he did best. The soft, soothing breeze moved around us, and I watched as Mom's shoulders and posture visibly relaxed.

"There's no rhyme or reason when it comes to people like the two of them," he said. "Nothing is gained from meanness and dishonesty."

Mom nodded and smiled at him.

"Mrs. Gray, I was wondering if you'd let me take Zoe to the deli in town for dinner," Adrian said, switching subjects seamlessly. "She tells me that's where kids sometimes hang out."

My eyes shot toward him, surprise and alarm rearing up inside me. I hadn't been to any of the regular social spots since our family fell apart. Would I even know how to act?

Adrian must've noticed my panicked expression, because he quickly added, "That is, if you want to go."

It occurred to me then that he was asking me on a date. Had even asked my mom permission. I'd be a terrible person if I said no.

"Of course." I looked at mom. "If it's okay with you."

She smiled, and I could see the wheels turning in her head. Dating was a normal teenage activity, and she'd been waiting for months to see me return to the regular ways of a high school girl. I figured she was also smart enough to realize that Adrian had been a good influence on me.

She had no idea how right she was.

She nodded "It's a school night, though, so be home early."

"No problem, Mrs. Gray," Adrian replied. "We'll just have dinner then head back here."

"Thanks Mom," I said, as Adrian made his way toward the driveway where his bike was parked, and I headed inside to drop by book bag and laptop in my room.

When I stepped out the front door, I noticed immediately that an extra helmet, white with some sort of writing on it, was strapped to his bike. He'd brought an extra helmet with him. On purpose. Obviously, he'd planned this date. The thought made my heart expand.

He handed the helmet to me, and upon closer inspection I saw the capital Z painted on the side. The bright yellow paint and the fancy script of the letter were decidedly feminine.

"I picked that up in Lexington last weekend," he said, reaching over to help me fasten the strap under my chin. "I figured you might like to have your own, since your going to be riding with me a lot."

His thoughtfulness overwhelmed me. I was astonished, not only because he'd purchased a helmet just for me but also because of what it signified.

A commitment. Wow.

"You are going to be riding with me a lot, aren't you?" he asked. I realized I'd been stunned into silence.

I didn't really trust my voice at that moment, but after such a wonderful gesture he deserved a response. I reached for his hands, which were busy strapping on his own helmet, and whispered, "Of course. And thank you."

He looked at me then, his eyes locking on to mine. The passion and strength in those baby blues nearly knocked me off my feet. My tongue was glued to the roof of my mouth, which wasn't necessarily a bad thing, because with the huge tidal wave of emotion crashing through me, there was no telling what might come out of my mouth if I tried to talk.

"Have fun, you two!" Mom called from the front porch, breaking the moment.

Adrian climbed on and I hopped up behind him, wrapping my arms around him as he eased the bike from the driveway to the road.

"Our first real date," he said, turning his head so I could hear.

I tightened my arms around his middle and snuggled close. As nervous as I was to walk into the deli where there would no doubt be lots of other kids, I was even happier to be with Adrian, knowing he wanted to be with me, too.

Deke's Deli was a locally owned sandwich shop on the corner of Main Street and South Rison Avenue. It had been around for as long as I could remember, and could be found packed with kids most summer afternoons thanks to the soft serve ice cream machine.

Adrian rolled to a stop in a parking spot in the far corner of the lot. I hopped off first and removed my new helmet. I still couldn't believe he'd gotten me my own, personalized helmet. Straightening, I ran my fingers through my hair to fluff up what the helmet had flattened out.

"I know I kind of ambushed you on the dinner thing," he said, taking both helmets and attaching them to the motorcycle seat with a bungee cord. "Didn't want to give you a chance to talk yourself out of it."

"I figured that." I grinned up at him.

"It'll be fine, you know." He reached for my hand, laced our fingers together, and headed toward the entrance.

Stepping through the front door at Deke's was just like I remembered it. The bell above the door dinged, and all the kids packed into the red vinyl booths turned to look at who had arrived. I smiled and waved at Nick Henry and Andrea Bishop, glad for at least a few familiar and friendly faces.

Nick's obvious affection for Andrea was probably the reason for his student government run.

As Adrian turned to walk toward an empty booth near the side window, red curly hair from the other side of the dining room caught my eye.

Vivian.

And Brett.

The desire to go over and talk to her came so naturally it startled me. It was like my heart didn't want to acknowledge what my mind knew... that Vivian didn't want to talk to me.

Viv turned and saw me, and I didn't look away. I just stared at her and hoped my sadness and contrition were evident in my expression. After a second, she turned back toward Brett without any reaction.

God, that hurt.

But it was my own fault, and I knew it.

Adrian squeezed my hand and gently tugged me to the empty booth. He didn't say anything. He slid into the seat beside me, rather than across, and draped his arm across my shoulder.

For a long moment we sat silent as activity buzzed all around us. I loved that he didn't try to make things better. He just let me feel my sadness.

But I knew that feeling sorry for myself wasn't going to help, so I took a deep breath and looked up at him, letting him know I was okay.

"Thanks," I whispered.

"Of course," he said, pressing a kiss to my forehead. "Ready to order?"

I nodded, rattling off my standard Deke's order of ham and provolone cheese on wheat, with lettuce and oil and vinegar dressing.

Adrian walked to the counter to order, and returned a moment later with our drinks. We sipped as we waited for our ticket number to be called.

"So, for our second date I was thinking a picnic," he said, sliding his arm across the back of the booth. "Down at the clearing."

My pulse picked up at the thought. Though we'd been to the clearing several times together, to plan something special was a different thing altogether. That he was intentionally arranging dates with me made my heart sing.

"That sounds wonderful," I answered. "When?"

"I was thinking on Saturday."

"Okay."

"And afterward," he said, lowering his voice and bending his head closer to my ear, "I can take you back. If you still want me to, that is. It's a private place where we won't be disturbed."

Before I could respond, the air turned clammy and a musty odor assaulted me. I knew what this was. I'd experienced it in the bathroom they day of Courtney's big announcement.

Without moving my body, I darted my eyes around the room, looking for the source of the change in atmosphere.

I found him near the cash register, leaned against the counter. His arms were folded across his chest, just as they'd been the last time.

He looked like my father. He was dressed like Dad, in khaki pants and a green polo shirt. But the look in his eyes sent chills down my spine.

His mouth quirked up on one side, as if mocking me, and he shook his head in a gesture of impatience.

The words sang through my head then, loud and clear.

It doesn't matter how much you try.

No! I would not give in to this trickery. This was not my father. Adrian had said so.

But as the image began to dissolve and the air began to clear, a voice deep inside me whispered that he'd been right.

It really didn't matter how much I tried. I would never be worthy of Adrian. And I would never be forgiven for all I'd done.

CHAPTER 23

O ur Saturday afternoon picnic at the clearing by the creek provided not only the perfect cover story for what Adrian and I were about to embark on, but also proved to be just as romantic as I'd imagined.

I forced myself to put away the thoughts of my father and the things his image had said to me. True or not, it wasn't fair for him to hold me hostage to those fears. Even though it might be difficult, I knew I had to try to fight my way out of the self-hatred I'd been steeping in all summer.

In the shade, the warm temperature didn't overwhelm us as we enjoyed our sandwiches, chips, and cookies. For the entirety of our meal, we avoided the subject of my dad.

We laughed. And it felt good.

"We were sitting in the middle of the cafeteria, with the entire junior class crowded into every available space, and I stood up to ask the presenter a question." Adrian leaned closer as I recounted one of my more embarrassing moments. "And Mitchell, who was my boyfriend at the time, pulled my chair out from under me. When I sat down, I landed right on my butt in the floor!"

Adrian laughed and his eyes danced with mischief. "I bet he was in the doghouse after that."

"I was so stunned, I didn't know what to say," I said, still laughing at the memory. "I just looked up at him from the floor and said *Mitch!* He said he'd meant to slide the chair back under me as I sat down, but one of his friends called his name and he looked away just as I started to sit."

"I would've enjoyed seeing that," Adrian cackled.

"You better not go back and revisit that moment!" I nudged him with my shoulder.

He shook his head. "Nah. Probably better in my imagination anyway."

The laughter made me feel lighter, stronger. Now was the time, with those feelings at the surface.

"So how do we do this?" I crumpled the wrapper from my cookie and tossed it back into the picnic basket Adrian's aunt had packed for us. "Like, hold hands or something?"

"We'll need to be touching, yes," he answered. "But we may as well be comfortable."

He reclined back on the blanket and opened his arms in invitation. Resting on my side, I aligned my body with his and laid my head against his chest. His arms came around me, and the breeze stirred around us, warm and calming, in that way I'd come to associate with his presence.

"Do you do that?" I whispered. "Make the wind stir like that?"

"It's one of my perks," he replied. "Helps people relax."

"Are you trying to hypnotize me?" I joked, my voice soft and quiet.

I felt the rumble of his chuckle beneath my cheek. "Just want you to be as chill as possible. I won't show you anything that will hurt you, and I promise nothing bad will happen to you. But it'll be pretty emotional. I want to be sure you're ready."

I closed my eyes and let his presence and the breeze that moved across my skin lull me into a peaceful state of mind.

I trusted him to take care of me, and to show me only things that would help me. "I'm ready."

The scene unfolded before us as if we'd just turned the page of a photo album. I took note of my surroundings. The parking lot of Pots and Plants, the local nursery. Lots of people loading up their cars with flowers for their spring landscaping. Two people not moving around, but standing still between two parked cars.

My dad and Courtney's mom.

Adrian held my hand, firm and secure, and pulled me closer. No one saw us, despite the fact they walked right by us. We were totally invisible to them, interlopers in a time that wasn't ours.

When we got within earshot of Dad and Courtney's mom Adrian pulled us to a stop.

"I've told Donna the truth, Mitzi," Dad said, his voice low but certain.

"But Jason," she complained.

"This," he whispered, pointed back and forth between the two of them, "was a mistake. A horrible mistake."

"Don't say that," Mitzi said, tears welling in her eyes. "It was special."

Dad sighed and shoved his hands in his pockets. "One encounter doesn't make a relationship. Certainly not a special one."

"But you were so happy." The pleading tone of her voice spoke of a desperation that was second nature to her. "We both were."

Dad shook his head. "No, I wasn't. And neither were you, if you're honest with yourself. It was a mistake. One I'm doing my best to put right."

This was not the man I'd seen in the dream or the visions. This man wouldn't laugh at my despair. This man wouldn't purposely jab at my deepest fears. *This* was the father I remembered.

But so much had changed, so much had happened. How could I be sure my hatred and spite hadn't turned the man I knew into a man who would forever be angry with me?

"She'll never forgive you," Mitzi spat, switching from the sad, doe-eyed begging to mean, nasty sniveling. "Not now that she knows you've been *elsewhere*."

"That's between my wife and me." Dad stood straight and looked Mitzi right in the eye. "I love my wife. I love my daughter. And I will go to the ends of the earth to make things right with them."

My throat clogged and tears filled my eyes. He loved me. He loved Mom. How could I ever doubt that? Suddenly I knew. I could choose which version of my dad to remember, to hold on to. I didn't have to accept that he was the bitter, malevolent person I'd seen in those visions.

And somewhere inside, I know I could make the same choice for myself. I could choose love over bitterness. Life over death.

Dad turned, and without another word, got in his car, and drove away. Leaving Mitzi stunned and speechless in the parking lot.

Before I even had a chance to process what I'd seen, Adrian and I appeared in my living room. I could tell from the clothes my mom was wearing that this was the day I'd dreamed about two nights ago. I breathed a sigh of relief that I wasn't going to witness the moment Dad first admitted everything to Mom.

I didn't think I could survive that.

Adrian's arm slipped around my waist, and I leaned into him, welcoming the sweetness of his presence.

"I'm still in shock, Jason," Mom said, tears spilling down her cheeks. "I just never imagined."

"I meant what I said," he replied, his voice laced with tenderness. "No excuses. I'm totally responsible for my actions. And I will work as long and as hard as I have to, to earn your trust again and put our family back together."

Mom nodded. "I believe you. I do. But I can't make you any promises. I don't know when, if, or how I'll ever be able to move beyond this."

"I know that, Donna. I'm not asking for promises. I just hope the door's not shut and locked yet. I know I don't deserve another chance, but I guess I'm selfish enough to ask for it anyway."

"You've done a lot of selfish things lately," Mom said. "But hoping for a chance to keep our family in tact isn't one of them."

"Does that mean you'll agree to counseling?"

Mom stood and walked over to the fireplace, her eyes fastened on the family photo sitting on the mantle. "We've spent a lot of years building this family. This *life*. I'm hurt and angry and betrayed, and my knee-jerk reaction is to tell you it's over forever. But I can't do that. There's too much invested to throw it away without trying." She took a deep breath and continued. "And despite it all, I still love you."

"I love you, too," Dad whispered, standing to walk toward her. He stopped short of touching her, as if he knew she would not accept it. "Always have and always will."

"When Zoe gets home we'll talk to her about counseling." Mom turned and walked toward the kitchen. "I'm sure we'll start out individually, but eventually she'll need to be involved. She's a part of this too."

"Yes, she is. And I know I've really damaged things with her."

"She's not going to be receptive toward the idea right now." Mom pulled a chair and sat down at the table. "But she'll come around. It will just take a while."

"As long as it takes," Dad said, dropping into the chair beside her. "As long as it takes."

Mom offered him a small smile, not a full-blown grin, but a hint of a pleasant expression that told me she believed him. Something in my heart lifted with that smile, caused the hope inside me to multiply.

Outside the house, I heard a car door that I knew was mine. Looking back once more at my parents, I saw them lock eyes and nod toward one another. Even in the midst of all the heartbreak, they were putting up a united front. For my sake.

Suddenly, I was in an unfamiliar place. A bank, by the looks of the long counter with several cubicle stations and people with their checkbooks in hand.

My dad sat across the desk from a man in a suit and tie.

"You want to close the entire account, Mr. Gray?"

"Yes," my dad answered. "And I'd like a cashier's check for the balance."

"Of course," the banker replied, opening a folder and reaching for a pen. "Do you mind me asking why you're closing the account?"

Dad shook his head. "Not at all. I was saving for a fishing trip to Canada with some friends next summer. But another expense has come up, so I'll just have to postpone the trip."

I knew about the trip he'd been saving for. He'd been talking about it for an entire year.

The moment seemed to fast-forward before my eyes, until I saw the banker hand my dad a check. The two of them stood, shook hands, and my dad walked out of the bank.

I felt Adrian's hand tighten on mine just before we jumped to a new place.

I recognized this scene as my dad's office, him sitting behind his desk. The phone was pressed to his ear, and I could hear his end of the conversation.

"Yes, anonymous," he said into the receiver. "If you have to, tell her that you re-filed with the insurance company and they reconsidered."

He waited a moment then said, "Thank you."

We flashed to a new place before I could blink. Mom sat at our kitchen table, some sort of bill open in front of her. She shook her head in disbelief and picked up her cell phone.

"I need to speak to someone in billing," she said.

I waited, hoping I would somehow be able to understand what was happening.

"This is Donna Gray," she began. "I received a statement that I no longer owe money for a biopsy I had in January, along with a refund check for the money I already paid toward the bill. I don't understand."

Biopsy? Did my mom have cancer? Fear slammed into me, hard and strong.

Adrian leaned close and whispered, even though I knew Mom wasn't going to be able to hear us. "Your mom had a biopsy of some skin on her back. Your parents didn't tell you because they didn't want you to be afraid. The lesion that was biopsied turned out to be benign. But the insurance didn't cover much of the cost, and the test was expensive."

"Is that even possible?" Mom asked, snapping my attention back to her. "For the insurance company to reconsider and decide to pay in full?"

It dawned on me then. Dad had taken his vacation savings and paid the bill for Mom's biopsy. Stepping closer, I looked for the date on the medical statement.

I felt tears fill my eyes as I realized the report was dated two days after Dad died. He'd done this just before the accident that took his life. And he hadn't wanted any credit for it.

I turned to Adrian and wrapped my arms around him. Closing my eyes, I held on tight.

And opened my eyes to the lush beauty of the clearing.

CHAPTER 24

I didn't sit up right away. The emotions were too fresh, and Adrian's arms were just too soothing. After a moment, I pushed myself up, pulling my knees to my chest and resting my chin atop them. I should say something. Thank him for showing me. Talk about what I'd seen. *Something.*

But I had no idea what to say.

Adrian saved me from babbling. "It's okay if you need to just be quiet and let it all sink in."

I nodded, took a deep breath, and told him the one thing I thought I could manage without crying. "I think it helped. No, I know it did."

Even after his enormous screw-up, my dad was still a hero.

"I'm glad." He reached for a strand of my hair, winding it around his finger as had become his habit.

"Can I ask you something?" I locked my gaze with his. "Something unrelated to what we just did."

"Of course. You can ask me anything."

"What happens after?" He looked puzzled, so I clarified. "After your job here is done. What happens? Do you just go away? Are you allowed to stay here? Do you have choices about college and your career?"

"I'm not really sure what happens after," he said, his fingers sliding along my jawline. "I'm sure the Boss isn't going to want me to be a high school dropout or anything."

He was being jovial. But I was seriously concerned. "I don't want you to have to go."

Adrian leaned closer, his hands finding my cheeks and cradling my face in his palms, causing my pulse to spike. He kept leaning until his our noses touched and his eyes seared into mine.

"He has a way of making sure things work out the way they're supposed to," he whispered, then closed the distance between us and melded his lips with mine.

I love you.

The words were right there, begging to burst free as we kissed in the shade of the trees. I wanted to say them. Badly. But a small part of me – the part that still wallowed in the misery I'd become accustomed to – screamed at me to stop.

Fear held me back. Fear of rejection? Fear of being unworthy? I wasn't sure, but I hated it. Hated the fear in a way I'd never thought possible.

I shoved the fear away, forcing it back to wherever it came from. Wrapping my arms around Adrian, I basked in this moment with him. He'd given me so much and asked for nothing in return. He'd given me back my life. Shown me how to forgive. Given me the chance to love again. I would not let the dark thoughts cloud my time with him.

And those three words… I tucked them away and held them in my heart. The moment would come, soon, and then I would give them to him.

CHAPTER 25

"I want to talk about Dad."

I could tell by the way Mom gripped the back of the kitchen chair that I'd surprised her.

Setting a pitcher of lemonade and two glasses on the table, I slid into my seat. We'd just returned home from church – a practice Mom had not let me get out of, despite my reckless summer – and were about to sit down for lunch.

"I'm glad," she said, dropping into her own seat. "And surprised. I'd begun to think you never would."

"It's still not easy." I poured my drink and stared at the yellow liquid, afraid if I looked at her I'd start crying before the conversation even got going. "I've dreamed about him lately."

"Oh Zoe," she whispered, reaching across the table to take my hand.

I kept going. "And I realize that I need to forgive him so that I can go on with life."

"Yes." Her voice cracked on the word.

"I'm still really angry. I feel betrayed. But I also feel so guilty for the way I treated him. The things I said.

Things I can never take back or apologize for because he's gone. And he wasn't a bad person. I know that. He made a bad choice, but he was a good man. And I loved him."

With that the tears ran down my cheeks and the lasagna on the table lost all appeal.

"I did too." Mom's grip on my hand grew tighter and in broken syllables she responded. "Just because he's gone doesn't mean you can't apologize. He knew you didn't mean those things, but if you need to say you're sorry, I believe he's listening and will hear you."

I nodded, unable to say much else. My chest heaved with sobs that had waited too long to escape.

Mom rose from her place and came around to my side of the table. Sitting in the seat next to me, she wrapped her arms around me and pulled me into her embrace.

How could I have forgotten how this felt? How a mother's arms could heal? How finding comfort with my Mom could ease the pain? And now that I'd finally let her share my grief, I couldn't stop the well of emotion that bubbled over.

She held me that way for what seemed like hours, while I cried every tear I'd held back since April. When the sobs began to subside, her shirt was soaked and my throat was dry, but her arms were still tight around me.

"I felt all those things too, Zoe," she said, her voice soft and warm. "I was so angry at him. Sometimes I still am. I was absolutely betrayed, and it felt horrible. And I've felt guilty. I said hurtful things to him, too. I said things out of anger that I didn't mean. I know you never heard them, because we never wanted you to see the ugliest part of things. But you need to know that you aren't the only one who said things and then regretted them."

"Could you have forgiven him?" I asked, my voice hoarse and weak.

She stroked her hand through my hair, the way she'd done when I was little. "I already had."

"How can you be sure?"

"Because I still loved him," she whispered. "I didn't trust him, and that would've taken a long time to rebuild, but I loved him. And I knew that as long as the love still existed that I could forgive. Maybe that would've meant that we worked things out eventually. I'd like to think so. But we'll never know."

"It's hard not knowing." I straightened, brushed my hair out of my face, and looked at her for the first time since the crying jag began.

"It is. Knowing he was willing to go the distance to try makes it a little easier. And I do believe that, Zoe. That he was sincere about doing whatever it took."

"I believe that, too," I whispered. "I believed it then. Before he died. I just didn't want to admit it."

"Your father made mistakes," she said. "Big ones. He hurt us. But we don't have to stay in that hurt forever. We can choose to live. We can choose to let life take us down new paths. We can choose joy."

"I'm getting there." I grabbed a napkin from the table and wiped the wetness from my cheeks.

"Does a certain handsome motorcycle rider have anything to do with that?"

"Yeah," I admitted. No sense denying it, although telling her the extent of Adrian's involvement in my return to the land of the living was probably not the best idea. "He makes me want to be better."

"Well, since that's the case, I can maybe get past the motorcycle."

She grinned at me and I laughed. She laughed, too, and I realized we'd just had our first normal mother-daughter moment since our world crashed down around us.

It felt good.

And I felt more whole than I had in a long time.

CHAPTER 26

Knocking on Vivian's front door wasn't easy. I had so much to atone for. I'd mistreated my best friend for months, and just when things were getting back to normal, I screwed it all up again.

She might not be ready to forgive me, but I needed to apologize so that at least she'd know how truly sorry I was.

The smile on her mom's face when she opened the door told me that Viv hadn't talked to her family about our falling out. It was possible she'd confided in her older brother, Jack. They'd always been close. But since he was off at college, I probably wouldn't run into him.

"Hi Mrs. Rogers," I said, forcing a smile even though I felt meek as a mouse.

"Zoe," she said, wrapping an arm around my shoulder and ushering me into the entryway of the house. "I'm so glad to see you. It's been too long."

I nodded. "I agree. Much too long."

"I hope you and your Mom are doing all right. I know these have been very difficult months."

"We're doing better," I answered. I felt a deep happiness at the honesty of those words.

"Vivian is upstairs in her room. Go on up."

With a smile and a whispered *thanks* I headed up the staircase. My hand grasped the polished wood of the banister, and with each step I forced myself to breathe normally.

Vivian's door was open, and as I approached her room I heard music and the clicking of computer keys. She was probably working on homework. I figured she wouldn't welcome my interruption, but I wouldn't take long. I'd say what I came to say and then leave.

Her desk faced the window, so as I stood in the doorway her back was to me. For a moment, I considered turning around and forgetting about everything, but I owed her more than that.

"Viv." I knocked softly before I lost my nerve.

She turned and said nothing. Just stared.

Well, I'd known it wouldn't be easy.

Stepping into the room, I shut the door behind me because no way did I want her mom overhearing.

"I won't stay long. I just came to apologize. For everything."

"Okay." She sounded skeptical.

"I know you probably won't believe me, but I wanted to talk to you. You were the only one I wanted to talk to about everything."

"Then why didn't you?" she asked, getting up from her seat at the computer desk to sit beside me on the bed.

"I'm not sure," I said, shrugging my shoulders and staring at the floor. "When Dad first came clean with

Mom and they told me they were separating for a while, my first instinct was to pick up the phone and call you. Then I started thinking about saying it all out loud, and…" I stopped before I choked on the words, and took a deep breath. "I was just so ashamed. So embarrassed. And I knew you wouldn't look down on me or anything like that, but I guess I thought if I just didn't talk about it, it would be like it wasn't real."

"I can understand that," Viv whispered. "I guess I can't really understand how you felt, but I can see why you didn't want to talk about it."

"Several times I almost told you, but I never had the guts."

"It's not really about guts," she said. "It's about your heart. It was broken. And I get that. I really do."

"Then, just when I thought maybe I could talk to you about everything, Dad died, and… I don't really know exactly how to put it… I just kind of fell down inside myself and tried to forget."

"And that's where Courtney and Nikki came in, right?"

I looked up at her then. I wanted her to see the truth in my eyes. "It was never about choosing them over you. *Never.* I wanted to forget, even if it was just for a little while. And I thought it was working. I thought the drinking and being reckless was helping. But it wasn't. In the end it just made things worse. I was ashamed of myself, because I knew the way I was acting was wrong. I avoided some of the guilty feelings by avoiding you.

And I'm so so sorry that I ever thought avoiding you was a good idea."

"I wasn't jealous of the two of them, you know?" A sad smile spread across her face. "As if I'd ever want to be anything like them. I knew what you were doing, and even though it hurt, I wasn't mad. I just hated the thoughts of you with those two."

"I never intended to tell Adrian the truth about my parents before you. It all just sort of happened by accident, before I even knew him very well. He found me out by the horse farm one night after I'd barely avoided a fight with Mom. Everything was just right at the surface. All the raw emotions. And I just blurted it out that Dad had an affair. Then once it was out there, I couldn't stop all the rest of it from coming out."

"And here's where I need to apologize to you," Viv said, shocking me.

"Why would you need to apologize to me?"

"For the way I acted at school the other day, after that scene with Courtney. I had no right to expect that you'd tell me all the details at all, much less before anyone else. This wasn't some piece of gossip. It was your life. Your family."

"I should've told you."

"In your own time," Viv replied. "My reaction was more about still being hurt about your summer with Nikki and Courtney than it was about you not telling me about your parents. For that, I'm sorry."

"So can we forgive each other?" I asked, a wave of hope bouncing around in my heart. "And maybe go back to rebuilding our friendship?"

Viv nodded. "Senior year. Let's move on and enjoy it."

We sealed it with a hug, and I hoped with all my heart that moving on from my own guilt and misery would be as easy as it was to move on in my friendship with Vivian.

"Brett asked me to go to the homecoming dance with him next month," she said. "And he held my hand in the parking lot yesterday."

"No way!" I hugged her again. "Tell me *everything*!"

CHAPTER 27

I hadn't realized I was dreading student government election speeches until I walked into school Monday morning. Public speaking had never been a fear for me, but somehow, in the chaos that had become my life over the past few weeks, I'd failed to consider how I would feel about standing up in front of the entire senior class and giving a speech. Especially now that everyone knew my dirty laundry.

Even though I was running unopposed for senior class secretary, I still had to give a speech. And really, it wasn't the winning or losing of the election that bothered me. It was wondering what they were all thinking of me while I was up there in front of them.

When I started imagining what might go through everyone's minds, I had to force myself to stop. The possibilities were just too upsetting.

Adrian joined me in the lobby, along with Vivian and Brett, and their presence alone was enough to calm me, even without Adrian's extra efforts.

He slipped his hand into mine, as if we walked hand in hand every day. The sweetness of his gesture overwhelmed me, and my heart swelled with the knowledge that he had let everyone know, very subtly, that he and I belonged to each other.

And that's exactly what I felt. A sense of belonging. He'd given me that. He'd given it back to me after my family trauma had obliterated it.

"Ready?" Vivian asked?

Responding to her proved difficult, because I realized that just as Adrian had given me a place to belong, Vivian had welcomed me back into a friendship I'd done nothing to deserve. Emotion clogged my throat as the reality of her love and support slammed into me.

So instead of talking, I simply put my arm around her shoulder and squeezed. Her smile let me know that she understood.

"You'll be great, Zoe," Brett said. His soft-spoken encouragement touched me, not because he was supporting me, but because it meant he cared for Vivian enough that he could look past my faults.

The senior class used the auditorium for student government speeches, while the other classes were spread out between the cafeteria, gym, and amphitheater. In the hallway outside the auditorium hung all the campaign posters, including the colorful ones Viv had made for me.

A group of students huddled to one side of the double doors caught my attention when they suddenly stopped their conversation and looked at me as I approached.

A glance at the poster beside them confirmed my worst fears.

"Zoe Gray for Class Secretery" was written in the middle, in sloppy black letters. The misspelling of *secretary* made me certain this was the work of Nikki and Courtney. Well, that and the pictures that surrounding the words.

Clearly, I'd been unaware that the two of them had snapped photos of me with their cell phones. Either that or I'd given my consent – while I was falling down drunk – for them to take pictures of me with a fifth of vodka turned up as I gulped it down.

My stomach lurched, and I felt sicker than I'd ever felt after drinking.

My confidence was already so tenuous. How in the world was I going to be able to stand up in front of everyone after this?

"Those nasty bitches!" Viv exclaimed. And loudly at that.

It was rare for her to curse out loud, and for a brief second I enjoyed the fact that she'd leapt to my defense. But it didn't change what had happened.

Adrian grabbed the paper from the wall, a rare expression of anger evident on his face. He crumpled the poster into a wad of paper, just Mr. Austin pushed through the crowd.

"Go inside and take your seats," he ordered the crowd that had been gawking at the evidence of my stupidity.

"Zoe, I'm so sorry," he said, stepping closer to me. "If I'd come down here sooner I could've removed that before anyone saw it."

"It's not your fault, Mr. Austin," I whispered, the words scratching my throat as I spoke.

"Don't let this stop you," he said. "I believe in you, regardless of whatever mistakes you made over the summer."

I nodded, completely unsure if I could take his advice. But his belief in me brought tears to my eyes nonetheless. He took the paper from Adrian and tossed it into the trash as he made his way into the auditorium and urged everyone into the seats.

"I'll save you guys seats," Brett said, quietly slipping into the auditorium.

Adrian turned to me then, when only he, Viv, and I remained in the hall. Taking my face between his palms, he put his face level with mine, stared directly into my eyes, and spoke.

"The girl in those pictures was *not* you. That was the girl who was suffering, searching for something to make her forget. That was the girl who'd lost her direction because of circumstances she didn't create and could not control. *You* are the real Zoe Gray. You are smart and kind and funny. You are sensitive and intuitive. And more than that, you have acknowledged your mistakes. You have *learned* from them. There is *no* shame in that."

"He's right, Zoe," Viv said, her voice soft as she laid a hand on my shoulder.

"You've come so far," Adrian said. "You've finally begun to understand what mercy and forgiveness can mean in your life. Don't let this petty, childish prank put a halt to all that you've accomplished."

I nodded because I couldn't speak. All at once, I found myself completely swamped by the goodness that surrounded me. Mr. Austin. Vivian. Adrian.

No way did I deserve their love or heir belief in me. I'd done nothing to earn any of it. But they gave it to me anyway.

I slipped my arms around both of them, pulling them to me for a group hug. A few deep breaths later, I stepped back and looked at them.

"Thank you." Completely inadequate words, but the only ones I could think of in that instant.

Reaching into my tote bag, I grabbed the index cards that contained my speech. Though I still felt unsure about myself, I would go through with it, if for no other reason than because of the people who'd just given me the most special gift I'd ever received.

Grace.

CHAPTER 28

I sat on the front row of the auditorium, sandwiched between Adrian and Vivian, pretending to listen to the speeches that preceded mine. In reality, I alternated between reading my index cards and staring at the maroon carpet that covered the floor.

"And now, our candidate for Senior Class Secretary, Zoe Gray." Mr. Austin's voice echoed throughout the room, boosted by the microphone at the podium on the stage.

Adrian squeezed my hand and said, "You can do this."

Vivian smiled, warm and kind, and whispered, "Show them who you are."

With a deep breath and a prayer that I could somehow remain standing and not collapse in front of everyone, I made my way to the podium.

Avoiding eye contact, I stared at my index cards and began to read.

"Fellow seniors. I'm Zoe Gray, and it has been my privilege to serve you in student government the past three years. Today I ask for your support to serve you once again, this time in the capacity of class secretary."

The words sounded ridiculous, asinine, even to my own ears. Everyone in the room knew I'd lost my father. Thanks to Courtney, they'd all heard about his affair. And after the poster in the hallway, there was not a doubt left as to how I'd dealt with it all.

It seemed pointless to continue to ignore it. Why not just acknowledge the truth?

There is no shame in that.

Adrian's words echoed in my mind, and I made a decision.

I put my cards down and looked out into the auditorium.

From somewhere deep inside me came a strength I didn't realize existed. In my heart bubbled a certainty that this was the absolute right thing to do. Whatever happened after this didn't matter. This was one more step in the process of my healing, and somehow I knew this step was a big one.

"There's no sense denying what all of you already know," I began, scanning my eyes across the students in the seats, making a point to linger on Nikki and Courtney. I wanted everyone in the room to know that I'd owned up to my mistakes and that I was through being ashamed because of them. "My father died in April, in a horrible car accident. It was the worst day of my life. After that, I withdrew from everyone and everything, including my best friend and my mother. I wanted nothing more than to forget how much I hurt. Over the course of the last week, I'm sure all of you have heard rumors about my parents. I won't dignify any of that gossip with a response, other than to say that my family's business is just that, *my family's* business. But I will acknowledge that I made mistakes in the wake of the tragedy that struck my family. I did things that I knew were wrong. Dangerous even. I made choices that were completely unbecoming of a student leader. I allowed grief and anger and guilt to take over. I let good judgment go out the window. I almost screwed up my life beyond repair. But I'm standing here before you a different person than the one who behaved so recklessly over the summer. A different person than the one you knew before the death of my father. I stand here today as a person who has made horrible mistakes. A person who has made terrible choices. But also as a person who has learned from those mistakes. A person who can own up to what she's done. A person who can say *I'm sorry.* And I *am* sorry. Sorry for disappointing the people who loved me and believed in me. Sorry for being such a lousy example. Sorry for dragging the people I love through such misery. So today, I'm not asking for your vote. I'm asking for your forgiveness."

My voice cracked on the last word, and, completely spent, I left the podium and returned to my seat, eternally grateful for Adrian's arm around my shoulder and Viv's hand gripping mine.

Let the chips fall where they would, but I was finished hiding from the truth.

I was scared to death. And exhilarated at the same time.

CHAPTER 29

"**S**o proud of you," Viv said, squeezing my hand as the rest of the seniors filed out of the auditorium. I was still glued to my seat after the emotional waterfall of coming clean in front of everyone.

Adrian's embrace had not faltered, and his arm still rested securely around my shoulders.

"Thanks, Viv," I whispered. "I'm so glad things are right between us again."

Mr. Austin approached, reaching out a hand. I stood up, forcing my legs to work, and shook his hand. The look of pride on his face filled my heart with happiness.

"Proud doesn't cover it," he said.

Tears welled in my eyes and I nodded, unable to respond for fear of erupting into a crying fit right there.

Vivian and Mr. Austin walked toward the double doors, leaving me alone with Adrian. We only had a moment before we'd be expected in our classrooms, but I needed to thank him.

"I couldn't have done this without you," I said, turning to face him. I grasped both his hands in mine, overcome all over again at the perfect rightness that enveloped me when we touched.

"You were brilliant." He leaned forward and pressed a kiss to my forehead. "Absolutely brilliant."

"I just told the truth."

"Sometimes that's the most brilliant, and most difficult, thing to do." His hand found my face and moved softly against my cheek. "I think my work here is almost done."

"Don't say that." Dread blasted through me and fear clogged my throat. I wasn't ready for him to go. "I still need you."

He smiled and brought his other hand to my face. "You need me less than you think you do. There's strength in you that you haven't even tapped into yet. You proved that today."

I shook my head. Regardless of how much I might be able to move forward on my own, the fact of the matter was that I just didn't want to be without Adrian.

I loved him.

"I wish I could tell him that I forgive him," I whispered, knowing he would realize I meant my father. "And that I could ask him to forgive me."

Adrian's head lowered, his intense gaze searching my eyes. "I think you're ready for that."

Ready? Ready for what? There was no way for me to talk to my father again. It was totally impossible.

Except that this was Adrian, the *Messenger*. Adrian who had taken me back to see things about my father that I'd needed to know. Adrian who could teleport. Adrian who could bring a calming breeze.

"You can do that?" My voice was almost non-existent, but I knew he heard me.

"It's tricky," he said. "And it's a skill we use sparingly. But for you, I believe it's exactly what you need."

"How?" I asked, my mind racing with questions and possibilities.

"Come on you two," Mr. Austin called, sticking his head back into the auditorium. "Time to get moving to your classes."

"Tonight," he said, pressing a soft kiss to my cheek. "At the clearing. I'll show you."

I emailed Lea as soon as I got home. I'd put it off long enough, and I was finally in a place where I felt like I could be honest about what had happened without sounding like a whiny child. Without going into the gritty details, I told her pretty much everything.

Dear Lea. I'm sorry I've been so out of touch. My family has been through a terrible crisis, and I just couldn't bring myself to talk (or type) about it. It's a long story, that began back in April, but I'll spare you the worst of it. Basically, my dad was unfaithful to my mom. He admitted it, and apparently it only happened once. He moved out, but he and Mom had decided to go to counseling and try to work things out. I was just angry. Livid, actually, and I refused to speak to him unless it was to tell him how much I hated him. Before our family counseling could even get started, Dad died in a car accident. Needless to say, it's been a long, difficult summer. But I'm finally recovering from the hurt I felt toward Dad and the guilt I felt because of my actions before he died. I've met a guy, a really wonderful guy, named Adrian. He's helped me through this in so many ways. I don't know what would've become of me if he hadn't stepped into my life. I know it was no accident that he came along when he did. I hope you'll forgive me for being so bad at writing. I will be better at it now. And let me know how Ruby is doing. I've been thinking about her. Love, Zoe.

I hit send and immediately felt a weight lift from me, as if by finally putting into words what I'd been through had given the events less power over me. Thinking back over the last few weeks, I had to admit that each time I'd opened up about things, the knot inside my chest had loosened.

Within minutes a new message from Lea appeared in my inbox. Given that Kenya was eight hours ahead of Kentucky, I was surprised.

Hello Zoe. We have a new computer at our home and I am up late surfing the internet because our connection is working well tonight. I am so very sorry to hear of all you have been through. I cannot imagine how much you have been hurt, and I completely understand why you have kept to yourself these last months. I will be praying for you, friend, and I'm very glad that you have found someone to share your burden. Angels are everywhere, Zoe, and it sounds as if you have found one. Please keep me posted on how you are. Even though we are separated by an ocean, I treasure our friendship. By the way, Ruby is doing much better! Much love, Lea.

Lea seemed to put everything in perspective. And though Adrian might not be an angel, he was pretty darn close.

I relayed the events of the day to my mom during dinner. My heart felt lighter than it had in months, and I found it surprisingly easy to share things with Mom, the way I had before everything fell apart.

"That must've been difficult," Mom said, stabbing a bite of chicken with her fork. "But I'm very proud of you."

"It was difficult at first, but the more I talked the easier it seemed. And when I finished, I was so relieved."

Tearing off a bite of buttery garlic bread, I thought of Adrian and our plans for later in the evening. Anticipation simmered inside me at both the thought of seeing him and the thrilling possibility of seeing my dad once more.

But I reminded myself that moments like this one between Mom and me had been so few and far between that I should enjoy it.

"I've been thinking about these," Mom said, reaching into her pocket and sliding my keys across the table toward me. "I thought you might like to have them back so you can drive to meet Adrian later."

I knew this was a major milestone. Mom had taken my keys after the first time she discovered I'd been out drinking with Nikki and Courtney. Cringing, I remembered how I'd acted when she confronted me, telling her I didn't *give a shit* what she said. I was so bound and determined to do whatever I wanted, no matter the repercussions. Looking back, I had no idea how she'd stayed so calm. Some super-secret Mom trick, I figured. She just looked at me, told me how much she loved me, and that she would do whatever she had to do to keep me safe.

"You may be dead set on defying me by taking part in this kind of dangerous behavior, but you will not drive your car under the influence," she'd said. I'll never forget the deep look of sadness in her eyes as she took my keys and dropped them in her pocket. "These are mine until further notice."

"Thank you," I whispered. Simple words and not nearly enough to express what I felt.

When I reached to pick up the keys, her hand covered mine and squeezed. The smile she gave me said more than any words about how far we'd come.

"Adrian's picking me up tonight," I said. "Is that okay?"

"I should be really worried about that motorcycle," Mom said, chuckling. "But for some reason I feel all right about it."

Yeah, he had a way of smoothing things out.

"He's always careful. And I wear a helmet. Actually, he bought me my very own." I cleared the dishes and loaded them in the dishwasher. "What time should I be home?"

I couldn't remember the last time I'd asked or cared about my curfew.

"It's a school night, so sometime before ten, okay?"

I nodded, happier than I would've imagined to be having this normal conversation with my mom.

I wished I could tell her what I'd learned about her medical bill. I was pretty sure she had no idea. It would've been the kind of thing she'd have told me as she tried to get me to open up about dad. Knowing what he did for her – for us – had given me so much peace, and I wanted her to feel it too.

Turning it over in my mind, I came up with a plan.

"Remember that fishing trip Dad was saving for?" I asked, snapping the dishwasher lid shut and turning it on.

Mom nodded. "He was so excited about it, even though it was a year away."

"Didn't he have a bank account set up?" I sat back down at the table. "Where he was keeping the money he saved?"

Mom's eyes narrowed, and I worried she would wonder how I'd known about the account. But the three of us lived in the same house, so if she asked, I'd just tell her I'd overheard something.

Which wouldn't exactly be untrue.

"He did," she replied, apparently unconcerned about my knowledge of Dad's savings. "But he closed the account a few days before he died. I assume he needed the money for living expenses since he'd been staying in Lexington after he moved out of the house."

"Surely Uncle Nolan wasn't charging him rent," I offered. I took a deep breath and continued with what I hoped would point her toward the truth of what he'd done with that money. "Maybe he paid off a debt or something."

She opened her mouth as if to object, but stopped. I watched her expression change as she worked her way back to those first few days after his funeral when everything was so chaotic.

And saw the moment the truth hit her.

Her eyes misted over and small smile played on her lips. "You know," she said with a heavy sigh. "I bet that's exactly what he did."

I heard Adrian's bike rumble into the driveway. He came to the door and exchanged the normal pleasantries with Mom, like the true gentleman he was. I could tell she was still elated from the revelation that Dad had paid that medical bill. My heart was joyous and full that after all she'd done for me, I'd been able to help her just a little.

I felt the soft breeze swirling around, lifting my hair off my shoulders, Mom, Adrian, and I talked on the front porch. His calming presence never ceased to amaze me.

Waving goodbye to Mom, I took my helmet Adrian that held for me and walked beside him toward the bike. I had no idea what I'd experience tonight.

The thought thrilled me.

CHAPTER 30

"How about a walk in the water before we start?" Adrian asked as we stepped out of the trees and into our clearing.

Our clearing. That's how I thought of this place now.

Smiling, I nodded. Adrian bent to unlace his boots and I kicked off my flip-flops. A moment later, jeans rolled almost to our knees, we stepped hand in hand into the cool water.

"Nice way to spend a late summer evening," he said.

"Very," I answered, leaning into him. "Kind of romantic."

"We haven't had enough of that." He kissed the top of my head. "I'm sorry for that."

"Not your fault." I shook my head. "Circumstances."

He pulled us to a stop, the pebbles slick and cool beneath my feet and water splashing gently around my ankles. The sun still shone bright behind the trees but dipped lower in the sky as sunset approached.

Adrian turned to face me. The look in his eyes left me breathless. His gaze was full of softness and longing. And did I dare to think it... love?

"I came here on assignment," he said, his voice thick with emotion. "I was supposed to help you forgive."

"You have." I stepped closer, grasping both his hands in mine.

"I never expected to fall in love with you."

Fireworks exploded inside my chest and my knees wobbled. Of all the things I thought he might say, I never imagined this. That he would say it first, in the moments before he would take me to see my father one last time. That he could even love me at all.

It was so beyond anything I deserved.

"It's muddied the waters a bit for me," he said. "Loving you and being assigned to you."

"Adrian, I —"

He stopped my reply with a touch of his finger to my lips. Just as well, since I had no idea what I was about to say. I wanted to tell him that I loved him, that he wasn't in this alone, that I was so grateful for every moment, every smile. There was so much inside me for him that I didn't even know where to start.

"I told you before that I've wondered about my motivations," he began. "When I manipulated time to go back and video Nikki putting those things in your locker, I was afraid I'd crossed the line. I did it because of my feelings for you, not just because of my assignment."

"Adrian, I need to tell you —"

He stopped me again. "But I realize now that anything done out of real love isn't selfish. I didn't do it to try to impress you or to make you like me more. I wasn't thinking about any personal benefit. The truth is, I'd have done it even if you hated me. Because I love you."

I felt a tear escape my eye, and I knew if I blinked more would roll down my cheeks. But I could not take my eyes off Adrian. The fierce look of love on his face and the sincerity of his words were stunning.

"When I talk about my Boss, you know who I mean, right?"

I nodded. Even if we'd never said it out loud, I knew. Adrian worked for God. As surreal as that sounded, I knew it was true.

"He's the most unselfish person there is. And he does great stuff for us all the time. He saves us from terrible things, and most of the time we don't even know it. He does all this not for any kind of personal gain, but because He loves us."

I nodded, and for the first time in my life I felt and understood the kind of love I'd always heard about, the kind of love Adrian was talking about.

"Real love isn't selfish," Adrian whispered. "It's selfless."

His heavy sigh let me know he was finished. Maybe now he'd let me talk. I reached up and twined my arms around his neck, tip-toeing to get my face closer to his. His arms circled my waist, helping me keep my balance on the slick stones beneath my toes.

"I don't know why you worried so much," I said, a smile spreading across my face. "You're the most selfless person I've ever known. And I love you, too."

His lips came down on mine, his arms tightening around me. Lifting me off my feet he twirled us there in the water, fast enough to make my head spin but slow enough to keep us upright. His lips never leaving mine, he walked us toward the creek bank.

As my toes touched the grass, Adrian lifted his head and just looked at me. Behind him, the sun sank lower and glowed a bright orange, the brilliant color creeping into the clearing through the branches of the trees that surrounded us.

Dusk, I thought. That time of the day when heaven seemed closest to earth. When anything was possible.

When love could bloom.

"I don't deserve you," I said.

"Don't say that." He lifted his hands to my face, threaded his fingers into my hair. "Never say that. You *do* deserve love. Everyone on this planet deserves love."

"I think I finally believe that," I said.

He smiled, resting his forehead against mine. "Are you ready to tell your dad that?"

"Yes." And I was. I really, really was.

CHAPTER 31

We sat facing one another, on the same blanket we used the last time we'd come here. Adrian held both my hands in his as he explained a bit about what would happen.

"I'm taking you to another plane of existence," he explained. "That sounds really fancy and official, but it's not really a place. Not physically anyway. If that makes any sense. It's sort of a realm between here and the afterlife."

I nodded my semi-understanding. As much as science and physics were not my thing, I'd watched enough science fiction on TV to know what he was talking about.

"This isn't a skill we use often," he continued, his thumbs stroking back and forth on my hands. "I've only seen my dad do this a couple of times."

Knowing that this skill was used sparingly made me all the more grateful that he was giving me this opportunity to tell my dad face to face that I'd forgiven him.

"We can't stay long, though," he cautioned. "I'm sure you're aware my Boss has people working against him. Crossing to different planes is one of the places that the enemy is able to intercept us, so to speak."

"Is it dangerous?" I asked, though the uncertainty would not be enough to stop me from doing this.

"Not really," he said, shaking his head. "The enemy can't touch you. You don't have to worry about being physically hurt or anything like that. But he can deceive you. That's what he does. He twists words and ideas until he deceives you into making a choice that's wrong."

"Sounds like I've had experience with him already," I said, thinking of my reckless summer.

Adrian nodded. "He used Nikki and Courtney to get to you. May have even been responsible for the upsetting visions you had of your father. But when we do this… when we cross to another plane, it's possible he'll approach you in a different way."

"How?" I whispered, wanting to somehow be as prepared as possible.

Adrian shrugged his shoulders. "It's not one specific way. Sometimes he'll appear as a random person you've never seen before. Sometimes he speaks through someone you know. Other times it's just an audible voice. If it happens, you'll know immediately that it's not part of what I've done. And I'll be right here." His hands squeezed mine. "I won't let you go."

"I can handle him." Nothing was going to keep me from seeing my dad one last time.

"We may not even encounter him," he said, leaning over to kiss my cheek. "That's what I'm praying for anyway."

"Me too," I said, sending up a prayer that all would be well. "I'm ready when you are."

"Here goes," he said with a wink.

A meadow appeared all around me. I could still feel myself sitting with Adrian in the clearing, but when I looked around I saw that I was standing in an open field. The grass was soft and cool on my bare feet. Even though he wasn't in the meadow with me, Adrian's gentle breeze moved across my skin, filling me with his soothing presence.

The sun blazed high in the sky, as bright as midday. Across the meadow a small stand of trees swayed in the gentle wind. As I watched their movement, a figure materialized in front of them. Almost translucent at first, the colors began to come into focus, details became visible, and before I could blink, my father was there, walking across the meadow toward me.

I couldn't move. Couldn't breath. My heart pounded and my mind raced. After all these months. All the hurt and all the guilt. He was here.

And he was smiling.

I wanted to weep, both for the joy of seeing him again and the sadness of knowing this was the very last time. How could I be given this gift but have it yanked away so quickly.

Yet still, I was so very grateful.

"Dad," I managed, before I broke into sobs and ran into his arms.

His arms pulled me in, his embrace warm and famil-iar. I wanted to stay there forever. Suddenly it didn't matter what he'd done or how badly I'd wanted to hate him. Regardless of all that, he was my dad, and I loved him.

"I'm so sorry," I said, burying my face in chest and struggling to get a hold of myself. "All those awful things I said. I didn't mean them."

"I know that, sweetheart." He pulled back and tilted my face up to his. "I always knew that."

"Dad, I don't have much time here."

"I know that, too," he said, his eyes softening. "Give Adrian my thanks for giving us this moment."

"I forgive you, Dad," I blurted, needing to say it worse than I needed to take my next breath. "For everything. I forgive you. Can you forgive me?"

"Of course, Zoe." He wrapped his arms around me again, placing a kiss on my temple the way he always used to. "Of course."

"I miss you so much."

"I've heard that you have someone new to help you with your math homework."

I felt the rumble of his laughter as he held me and my heart was simultaneously joyful and broken.

"You're a wonderful young lady, sweetheart," he said. "And you're going to be an amazing woman. I'll be watching the whole time."

"I can't believe this is the last time I'll ever see you."

"Be glad we had this time," he squeezed me tighter. "I am. I'll be with you every moment."

He stepped back, smiling at me as his form began to fade away.

"I'm so proud of you," he said, fading more with each second. "And I love you so much."

"I love you, Dad."

He smiled once more, and then he was gone.

Falling to my knees I gave over to the torrent of tears that had never truly subsided. Adrian waited for me in the clearing, and though I could feel his presence, I knew he was giving me this moment to grieve.

Sadness coursed through me. The kind of sadness I hadn't allowed myself when Dad died. The natural sadness that followed the death of a loved one, rather than the bitter, toxic kind I'd wallowed in at the time. But even through the sadness, I felt the unburdening of my spirit, the heaviness being replaced by a lightness that I'd not known in months.

Adrian's words returned to me then. *You forgive for yourself, for your own well-being. Love can't grow where bitterness takes root.*

He'd been right. I felt love begin to fill the emptiness that had ached inside me for so long. Love for my dad. For mom. For Adrian. The love had been there all along, but my guilt and hatred had hidden it.

Now it had room to grow.

Though I knew a part of me would always be sad for the loss of my father, I knew I was ready to return to Adrian and begin the process of going on with life the way Dad wanted me to. The way *I* wanted to.

I got back on my feet and took a deep breath. Just as I was about to ask Adrian to bring me back a loud cracking noise thundered through the meadow.

I looked around, confused and uncertain, and noticed the earth splitting in front of my feet. I jumped backward, afraid that the hole in the ground would swallow me. The deafening splintering continued, growing so loud I covered my ears and slammed my eyes shut.

"Zoe," said a familiar voice.

Opening my eyes, I saw that what had been a peaceful, serene meadow was now a wide chasm, so deep the bottom could not be seen. Jagged edges of the ground jutted out in front of me, and I wondered if hell was what lay at the bottom of the pit.

A movement to my right caught my eye, and I turned to see the source of the voice, shock slamming me in the chest.

"Courtney?"

CHAPTER 32

How could she be here? Though everything about her seemed normal, a dark and ominous shadow darkened her form.

"In body, yes," she replied in a voice that sounded like hers, but was somehow different, more sinister. "In spirit, not so much. I am the *Inhabiter.*"

Just as Adrian told me, I realized immediately that this was not part of what he was showing me. Not part of his plan. Though I could no longer see the clearing, I reached back into my mind, pictured the two of us as I knew we were, sitting on the blanket holding hands. Focusing on the physical sensations, I felt his hands grip mine, tight and secure. His strength seeped into me, and I found the fortitude to continue.

"Who are you?" I breathed, not exactly sure if I wanted an answer.

"You know who I am!" This time, the voice that roared from Courtney's throat was not hers, and a chill ran up my spine. "I'm the one who can give you your father back."

My heart lurched then seemed to stop altogether. What this *inhabiter* said was not possible. My father was dead. If there was a way to bring him back, Adrian would've told me.

"Your little *Messenger* didn't tell you that, did he?" the voice inside Courtney sneered. "Of course he didn't. His kind aren't ones to offer you what you actually want."

Could it be true? My mind raced with the possibility and I struggled to maintain my balance.

"All you have to do is wish it," the *inhabiter* said, the voice now a smooth, inviting tone. "Just say the words, and I can make it happen."

Pictures bombarded my mind. Dad at my graduation. Dad walking me down the aisle at my wedding. Dad with my children, delighting in being a grandfather. Dad reunited with Mom, living their golden years together.

Was it really true? Could I have those things?

"Zoe." Adrian appeared on my left, a bright, glowing light surrounding him, so different from the shadows that darkened Courtney's presence. His eyes fixed on me with an intensity I'd never seen.

"Is this true?" I whispered.

"In a way, yes." He stepped closer, lowering his voice. "To accomplish it time would have to be manipulated and changed. I've told you that is a tricky thing, something we use sparingly and only for the good of the person we're helping. In the hands of one working from the opposite side, the ramifications would be unthinkable."

"How could it be bad to have my father back?" I asked, my voice pleading and desperate.

"It's not that simple," Adrian said.

"But it is," hissed the voice of whatever was inside Courtney. "Say the words and it will be so."

My father took form again, across the chasm from me. He looked entirely different than before, this time dressed in black from head to toe.

"I can come back to you," his voice called to me. Though he was far away, I could hear him as if he stood right next to me. "Say the words and time will return to the day of my death, except I will not die. The accident that took my life will not occur."

His voice sounded different. *Off* somehow. It reminded me of when he'd laughed at me in the school bathroom, while I sat devastated and broken.

Courtney or whoever she was at this moment stepped toward me. "This weak-minded child has been *inhabited,* to offer you this chance."

I looked at Adrian and begged with my eyes for him to tell me something that made sense. Somewhere in my mind I knew that the *inhabiter* was pure evil, but how could I say no to the very thing my heart desired? Would I ever recover from it? Or would I live with a new kind of guilt for the rest of my life?

"Look at him," he said, point across the chasm to the figure of my father. "Really look at him. You've seen him before. In the bathroom and again at Deke's." Stepping so close our noses practically touched, Adrian whispered to me in a voice so impassioned that I couldn't have taken my eyes from him if I tried. "If you do this, everything since that day will be erased. *Everything.* Your father will still be alive, but nothing that's happened since then will be the same. The forgiveness you worked so hard for? Gone. The mend in the relationship with your Mom? Evaporated. Me? I will never have come to Rison. You won't remember me. You'll never even have known me." His eyes became glassy with unshed tears as he whispered his next words. "But I will *always* remember you."

My insides seemed to tear in half, ripping and shredding my soul in the process. Choose my father and lose Adrian? Choose Adrian and give up the chance to have my dad back? How could I make a choice like this? The thought of either caused more pain than I'd ever imagined was possible.

Tears streamed down my face, the questions playing relentlessly in my mind. I couldn't even give voice to the pain blazing inside me.

"My heart wants to beg you not to do this, not to leave me," he said, blinking in an unsuccessful attempt to keep the tears from falling. "But I won't play with your emotions that way. I can only tell you, in as unselfish a way as I know how, that manipulating time this way can have far reaching consequences. Repercussions that can echo forever, and completely change the fabric of our existence."

"Don't let him fool you." My father's voice echoed from across the chasm, booming in my ears and zinging along my nerves. "His intentions are not honorable. He only wants you for himself."

Something wasn't right. The voice was my dad's, but the words didn't sound like him, and the motivation behind them felt wrong.

"Remember what I told you, Zoe," Adrian said. "The *inhabiter* deceives."

I closed my eyes, all at once unable to process one more thought. Somewhere in all this chaos was the truth. I just had to find it.

"Zoe, listen closely." My father's voice. Not the one from the other side of the massive crack in the ground, but the one I'd just heard as we said our last goodbye. His words were as clear as anything I'd ever heard, except that I wasn't hearing them. They were in my head, as if he could somehow communicate with me in thought.

"Keep your eyes closed and don't say anything," he said. "Don't let them know I'm talking to you. That *thing* inside Courtney is evil. You have to know that. And it isn't telling you the whole truth. Adrian has warned you about the dangers of manipulating time. It's so much worse than either of you could imagine. I've seen the possibilities, Zoe. That projection of me standing across the chasm from you? That's the me that would return. Surely you can see he's not the same. And think back on the day I died, before you found out I was gone. Do you remember how you felt about me? You were so angry, rightfully so. *That's* what you'd go back to. You'd still be furious with me, simmering with all that anger and disgust. You'd be right back where you started. So would your mother. And how long do you think it would take you to forgive me if I was like that imitation over there? Could you ever? Would I even try to earn your forgiveness as that egotistical imposter? What would happen to you if I treated you with callousness and never earned your forgiveness? What would become of you if you had to live with that hatred for the rest of your life? *That's* what the *inhabiter* wants. He wants you to trade your life for what you *think* you want most."

Dad's voice fell silent but I could still feel him there, inside my mind. Trying to sort through all that was swirling in my brain, I did what he said and thought back to the day he died. I'd woken that morning the same way I had each morning since he split our family apart with his infidelity. Angry and hostile, lashing out at anyone and anything. Swearing I'd never forgive him. Not caring about a single thing in my life.

If I returned to *that*, would I ever move beyond it? Especially if Dad was right and the version of him in all black standing on the other side of the chasm was the one who came back? And could I really send Mom back to that place of such betrayal and devastation?

"I'm not telling you my death was designed for some great purpose. That's not how things work. It wasn't a pre-planned destiny for me to die and leave you fatherless, with all this baggage to overcome." Dad's voice spoke again to the thoughts racing through my mind. "But I've seen that purpose can be given to even the worst of circumstances and that good can come from things that began as mistakes. That's how good Adrian's

Boss is. Tell the *inhabiter* that you will not change this destiny. It's the right thing to do."

Doubt fled. *This* was my father. The one who would sacrifice his own life for my happiness and well-being. When it mattered most, Dad had been there for me, to help me make the most important decision of my life.

Resolve filled me. Opening my eyes, I turned to Courtney's form, stared into the eyes of the evil inside her, and spoke the words my dad had instructed.

"I will not change this destiny."

CHAPTER 33

Thunder exploded in the meadow, and the imposter of my father disappeared in a burst of black smoke. The ground shifted violently beneath my feet, and I struggled to keep my balance as the enormous crack began to close.

Courtney's form went limp and would've fallen to the ground had Adrian not appeared behind her. He grabbed her and flashed immediately out of view, both of them vanishing from the meadow which was quickly returning to the way it had looked when the vision began.

Seconds later, Adrian returned as the last of the chasm closed, the ground looking like nothing had ever disturbed it.

"I took her home," he said. "She won't remember any of this."

I nodded, still in shock from the events that just took place. He stepped toward me and wrapped his arms around me, holding so tight I could barely breathe.

Not that I wanted to. At this moment, I needed him to hold me more than I needed to take in oxygen.

A rustling in the grass beside us caught our attention. We both looked up, though his arms did not leave me, and watched as my father took form in front of us.

He smiled at me, the kind of smile that tells a daughter's heart all she needs to know about her father's love. To Adrian he nodded, as if to say he approved.

"Thank you," Adrian whispered, his voice stumbling over the words as emotion got the better of him. "I'll always take care of her. I promise."

"You saved me, Dad," I said, drawing his gaze back to me. "I love you."

He smiled again and lifted his hand to wave, as his form began to shimmer and dissipate. I waved back as I watched him disappear. I knew it was the last time.

In the next moment, Adrian and I were back in the clearing, the meadow and all that it had contained erased from my sight. I was in his lap, plastered against him, as our arms tangled in our attempt to stay close. The tiniest strip of orange light glowed at the horizon, reflecting in the water of the creek.

I had no idea what to do or how to proceed. I felt too much to say anything.

Adrian's hands moved to my face, cupping my cheeks and bringing me eye-to-eye with him.

"You were so strong," he said, kissing my forehead then both cheeks. "So brave."

His lips found mine, fierce and intense, blazing with the emotion of all we'd just experienced.

"I'm so proud of you," he said, pulling back to look at me once again. "And I'm so sorry."

"Sorry?" It was all I could mutter after he'd just stolen my breath with that kiss.

"I should've done more to warn you," he said. "Should've told you how evil could inhabit someone familiar."

"How could you have known what would happen?" I whispered, finally finding the rest of my voice.

He shook his head. "And I should've gone to the meadow with you in the first place. I wanted to give you privacy, but I should've gone. I should've been more careful. I knew something like this was possible."

He was blaming himself, allowing guilt to creep in. I knew first hand the damage that could do.

"Stop this," I ordered, taking his face in my hands the same way he'd done to me. "You know how you've been telling me for weeks that I've got to get over all this guilt and forgive myself? Well, don't you fall into that same trap."

"But —"

I stopped him with a finger on his lips. "You gave me what I thought I'd never have. Closure with my dad. Yes, the *inhabiter* tried to sway me, but you were there, along with my dad, to help me make the right choice."

I pressed a soft kiss to his lips, bringing tenderness to a moment that had become unbearably intense. "And you succeeded. Look around us. Look at me."

His blue eyes fastened on mine, a lock of beautiful ebony hair falling across his forehead, and what lived and breathed inside me for him grew inexplicably deeper.

"I love you so much," he whispered, his voice throaty and gruff. "If I'd lost you –"

"You didn't," I said. "I'm here to stay."

"I was so afraid I'd fail you."

"Your first assignment was a success." I tilted my head and grinned at him.

"You know you're more than an assignment," he said, pushing a strand of my hair behind my ear. "So much more."

"Are you going to get a new assignment now?"

"I haven't been given anything yet, so I figure I'm staying put. At least for a while."

"Do you need a partner?" I asked, my voice coy even though I desperately wanted him to say yes.

"I'll always need you." He kissed me, his lips slow and soft, completely unhurried. "Always."

CHAPTER 34

It seemed my first class would never be over. I wasn't sure if I wanted it to hurry up and end or to drag on forever. Second period was the senior class ceremony in the auditorium, and I couldn't decide how to feel about it.

The results of student government elections had been tabulated. Even though I was running unopposed for class secretary, I'd still be announced, along with the others who'd been elected to class offices, in front of the entire senior class.

Inside I felt solid and renewed, but as I remembered the way I'd spilled my guts during my speech, I couldn't help but be a bit nervous about getting up in front of everyone again.

"Stop fidgeting," Vivian whispered. "It's all going to be fine."

I smiled, grateful all over again for my reconciled friendship with Viv. I was just about to respond when the intercom beeped.

"Faculty, students," came Principal Burton's voice. "We are now under lockdown procedure. There is no emergency, but students should remain in classrooms and all doors should be locked until this lockdown is over. Thank you."

I cut my eyes toward Viv.

"Drug dogs," she whispered.

I nodded, figuring she was right.

Once or twice every school year, law enforcement officials brought drug-sniffing dogs into the school. Students never knew when they were coming, and we always went into lockdown mode so that no one had a chance to run to their locker, grab their stash, and flush it down the toilet.

Through the small, rectangular window on the door I caught a glimpse of a small group of people walking down the hall. Other students noticed as well, which prompted the whispering and speculating to begin.

"Let's get back to work," Mrs. Harvey instructed. "I'm sure we're all aware of the reason for the lockdown, but you still have an assignment to complete."

With nothing to do but go on about business, I turned my attention toward my writing assignment and tried not to totally stress out about the student government ceremony next period.

Mrs. Harvey was cool about letting us have our cell phones on our desks, as long as we did our work instead of wasting time. As I continued writing about the nature of Lennie and George's friendship in *Of Mice and Men,* I kept up with the time by glancing at my phone. Counting the minutes until the ceremony was stupid, but I couldn't help myself.

The flash of an incoming text caught my eye and I looked at my screen.

Adrian.

Hope the lockdown doesn't cut into next period. Anxious to see you accept your student gov't office.

Smiling, I considered replying, but thought better of it as Mrs. Harvey made her way down my row in her normal classroom patrol.

I was just putting the finishing touches on my essay when the intercom beep sounded again.

"The lockdown is now over," Principal Burton said. "At the end of first period, all seniors should report to the auditorium so that we may begin the student government assembly as quickly as possible."

A moment later, the bell rang, and I handed my paper to Mrs. Harvey. She patted me on the back and told me she was very proud of the speech I'd made at the election assembly. Smiling, I thanked her. I already felt brand new on the inside, and I hoped the student government ceremony would be the start of a new chapter for me here at school.

Grabbing my things, I headed toward the auditorium.

CHAPTER 35

Halfway down the hall, Adrian fell into step beside me. His arm draped across my shoulders, his warmth surrounding me.

"Hey there," he said, pulling me closer. "Nervous?"

I looked up at him. "How'd you guess?"

"I'm good like that." He winked.

Amazing how just a few words from him could easy my anxiety.

"Got your acceptance speech ready?"

"Yep. It's short and sweet." I reached into the side pocket of my backpack to retrieve my note cards, only to find it empty.

Thinking back on my drive to school – in my own car, which I now had the keys to – I remembered dropping them onto the passenger seat.

"I left my speech in the car," I said. "Can you go on to the auditorium and tell Mr. Austin I'll be right there."

"No problem," he answered, sliding the backpack off my shoulder. "I'll take this and save you a seat."

I hurried to the front door and around to the side parking lot. As I made my way to the second row of spaces, I noticed police cars in the back corner of the lot across the street. A handful of what I assumed to be students were huddled together near one of the cruisers, hands cuffed behind their backs.

I figured I probably wasn't supposed to see the results of the drug dogs' trip through our school, so I moved quicker on the way to my car, intending to get back to the auditorium as soon as I could.

Reaching into the passenger seat for my note cards, a shrill voice rang out from across the street.

"As soon as I call my father, he'll make all this go away!"

Nikki.

I straightened, and looked toward the commotion. I knew I shouldn't stare, but I couldn't stop myself. Several of the handcuffed kids were known drug users. Some had even been caught before.

Seeing Nikki and Courtney among them was a surprise. Not because they were so much more virtuous, but because they were more conniving. And I'd thought Nikki at least was smart enough to not bring her drugs to school.

Her defiance was obvious in her stance, even from this distance. Unlike Courtney, Nikki was already eighteen, so depending on what sort of drugs they found in her possession these charges could be very serious for her.

"Young lady, your father is welcome to come down to the station and we'll explain the charges to him." I heard the officer's loud, booming voice clearly, as he led her to a squad car and ushered her into the backseat.

Flashing back to the night of the accident, I was sobered once more to realize that I could've been in that exact predicament. If not for Adrian, I would've been in the back of the police car that night. And heaven knows what else I might've gotten myself into if I'd continued down that dangerous path.

I said a silent prayer of thanksgiving that, with help, I'd managed to pull myself out of that mire. I would never take my good fortune for granted again. And I would never again gamble with my life.

CHAPTER 36

I sank down into the seat between Adrian and Vivian just as Mr. Austin stepped up to the stage to begin the ceremony.

"You'll never guess what I saw in the parking lot," I whispered.

Adrian leaned toward me as Viv did the same.

"Nikki and Courtney were handcuffed. I saw them being put into police cars in the lot across the street."

"Everyone's talking about it," Viv said, her voice hushed as Mr. Austin began to speak. "They're saying the dogs found marijuana and pills in their lockers, and more in their pockets once they escorted them out of the building."

Adrian's hand gripped mine, as if he knew I was thinking back on my disastrous summer and how close I'd come to being in the thick of it with Nikki and Courtney.

Brett, who sat on Viv's other side, leaned over. "They've had it coming for a long time. Nikki's been supplying pills to people for over a year. Glad she finally got caught."

With the kind of money her parents gave her, I'm sure Nikki had found any number of unscrupulous people who sold her drugs, which she then turned around and sold for profit to kids at school. I'd been cavorting with a drug dealer all summer. The potential for lasting repercussions and outright tragedy had been immense, and I was overwhelmed yet again to know that somehow I'd escaped all that insanity intact.

We settled in to listen as Mr. Austin began his announcements.

"In the position of Administrative Liason, I'm proud to announce a newcomer to student government, Nick Henry."

Applause rang out as Nick moved to take his place in the fifth seat on the stage. Secretary was the next office to be announced. I took a deep breath and squeezed Adrian's hand.

He leaned over, lips to my ear, and whispered, "I love you."

Before I could even respond, Mr. Austin continued.

"Zoe Gray, running unopposed for Secretary, returns to student government after serving as your president for the last three years."

I took note of the clapping as I made my way to my seat next to Nick. No tomatoes were thrown, and no boos were shouted, so perhaps I was in the clear.

"Your new Vice President for Class Activities, Carla Mabry."

"Congratulations," I said as Carla sat down beside me.

"Thanks," she said, smiling.

So far, so good I thought to myself.

Andrea Bishop took her seat next to Carla after being announced as Vice President for Publicity, followed by Daniel Williams as our new Class President.

Once the officers were seated, Mr. Austin invited Nick to the podium to make his acceptance speech.

I tried to listen, truly. But my pulse pounded so hard in my ears I could barely hear. The last time I'd stood at that podium I'd laid myself bare, and here I was about to step up to it again. My eyes sought Adrian, only to find him smiling. Around me air started to stir, and I felt the soothing calm begin to seep in. He'd seen my panic and given me his comfort.

Talk about thankfulness.

"And now, your class secretary, Zoe Gray," Mr. Austin announced, turning to smile at me as I stood.

Stepping up to the microphone, I gripped my note cards in my sweaty hands. I'd spent some time thinking about what to say, and without any big revelation to share, I planned on sticking to my script this time.

"I've learned a lot about grace and forgiveness over the past few weeks," I began, looking around the room to the people who mattered most to me. Mr. Austin. Vivian. Adrian. "And I've learned a lot about second chances. I thought I didn't deserve any of those things, but thanks to my friends and loved ones, I've learned that everyone deserves a second chance. I've been given a second chance, not only as a member of student government, but as a part of this school and community.

I want all of you to know that I'm grateful. And that I will not waste it. Thank you."

I stepped back from the podium, ready to return to my seat, when I saw it begin. People were standing. Whole groups of students rising to their feet at once, until everyone in the auditorium stood.

And then they started clapping.

It took a few seconds to realize what was happening.

A standing ovation. They were giving me a standing ovation.

A movement near the door to the auditorium caught my eye. Glancing over, I saw my mom, clapping and crying, looking up at me with such pride in her eyes.

It had been so long since I'd felt like she was proud of me, and I promised myself I would never again give her reason to doubt me.

She waved at me and I smiled back, as a tear spilled down my cheek. This time the tear wasn't full of sadness, but rather joy and accomplishment.

Scanning for Vivian, I found her not only clapping but jumping up and down. How had I ever thought I could do without her exuberant friendship?

And then my eyes landed on Adrian. The one who brought me out of the darkness. The one who brought me back to life and filled that life with happiness.

"Love you," he mouthed, his clear blue eyes staring up at me with a love so deep and profound I knew I'd done nothing to earn it.

He was God's gift to me. And I would cherish him always.

EPILOGUE

A drian and I sat at the picnic table in my back yard after dinner one evening in April, seven months after that day in the auditorium. After a typical Kentucky winter of seemingly endless cold, gray days, spring was beginning to make its appearance. We took advantage of the warm evening to resume our habit of homework at the picnic table.

We'd each already been accepted to the University of Kentucky. I had plans to study history and government, while Adrian planned to major in mathematics. Since our acceptance letters came in December, we'd gone about making plans for college under the assumption that Adrian would be able to go.

Even though Adrian was sure his Boss wouldn't separate us, I still worried. A new assignment could come down at any time, and the thought of Adrian leaving made me feel sick to my stomach.

Homework finished, I slid my notebook into my backpack. When I turned back to Adrian, he was holding an envelope. His name and address were printed neatly on the front, with no return address in the corner. He stared at it without looking at me, and my stomach sank to the soles of my feet.

This was it. A new assignment. He was going to have to go away.

Could I follow? Maybe there was a college close enough to where he'd be that I could attend.

"This was waiting for me when I got home," he said, his voice almost a whisper. "I recognized it right away."

I swallowed hard. "What does it say?"

"I don't know yet." He shrugged his shoulders. "I wanted to wait and open it with you."

I reached for his hand, wrapping my fingers around his. "Whatever it is, we will be okay." Even though the thought of being apart killed me, I knew in my heart that nothing would change the way we felt for each other.

Adrian nodded and tore open the envelope.

He pulled me closer so we could read together. Taking a deep breath, I looked at the words that could change everything.

Adrian Shaw:

A new assignment has been given to you. It begins in August of this year. In your dormitory, on the floor you've been assigned, you will find a young man named Chase. This young man is recovering from an addiction to prescription pain pills, and will need support and guidance as he is away from home and his family for the first time. There is no end date to this assignment, as it is our plan for the two of you to remain friends and for you to help him stay grounded and steadfast throughout your time at the University of Kentucky. Remember to ask if you and your partner need assistance or resources.

I burst out laughing as joy bloomed inside me. Although Adrian had been so sure, in the moments before he'd opened that envelope, I'd seen the concern in his eyes.

But he'd been right all along.

We weren't going to be separated!

And I was his partner. The letter said so.

Adrian jumped up from the table, pulling me with him. He wrapped his arms around me, and lifted me off my feet.

"I knew it!" he said, spinning us in circles.

"I'm so happy," I said, giggling as he slowed, gently setting my feet back on the ground. "I think this is why you were assigned to me. Not just so you could help me or so that we could fall in love, but so that I could work with you. I know I'm not a *Messenger,* but I think your Boss had a purpose for me, too. To be your partner."

"You're absolutely right," he said, kissing my forehead. "Wherever we go, whatever we do, we'll be together."

"Always," I whispered, gazing deep into his baby blues. Behind him the sun glowed orange on the horizon, lighting the sky with brilliance before it disappeared for the night.

Dusk, I thought. How appropriate.

"Always," he whispered, bringing his lips to mine. "Always."

THE END

A Note From the Author

If you enjoyed this book, please consider leaving a review at your place of purchase and/or any other online review site you frequent. Customer reviews are one of the best ways to show an author you enjoyed his or her work and can be invaluable for other readers as they browse for reading material. This author reads all reviews and greatly appreciates each one.

About the Author

Amy Durham discovered her love of writing in the sixth grade. What began as a love of writing poetry soon turned into stories scribbled into school notebooks. In the eighth grade, her English teacher told her she was good at it and encouraged her to continue to put pen to paper. At that moment, the die was cast, and writing would forever be a part of her life.

As an adult, Amy focuses her efforts on writing Young Adult Fiction… adventure, romance, and life-lessons… woven together as imagination and escape for young readers. Amy holds a firm belief that books are not only entertaining, but have the ability to transform young lives. A book can educate. A book can teach compassion and kindness. A book can spark interest. A book can be a companion. Simply put, books can accompany and guide young readers as they try to navigate their way through the twisted, confusing roads of adolescence.

She lives in Kentucky, where she is a middle school teacher. She and her husband are raising three wild, intelligent, and creative boys, giving her plenty of fodder for the love and adventure she enjoys putting in her stories!

Amy loves to hear from readers. You can contact her at:

amybdurham@gmail.com
www.amydurham.com
twitter.com/Amy_Durham
facebook.com/AuthorAmyDurham

Turn the page for a sneak peak at *For Once: A Sky Cove Short Story*, coming soon from Amy Durham.

Coming Soon

For Once: A Sky Cove Short Story

Netfilx online streaming was the cause of my insomnia. And if I wasn't careful it would be the cause of my GPA plummeting. I looked at the clock and almost cursed the day I discovered *Dr. Quinn*. Almost, but not quite.

I smiled, replaying the moment that Sully finally told Dr. Mike that he loved her, right before they jumped off the cliff and into the river to escape her captors. How romantic was that? And how pitiful was I that my crazy romanticism had me up at all hours of the night watching old TV shows because my own life was so totally void of anything close to romance?

Sighing, I laid my glasses aside, shut my laptop, and snuggled down under the covers. January in Maine was brutal and required at least twenty pounds of cover on the bed. Looking at the clock, I groaned. At 2:00 a.m., I could still manage about four hours of sleep before I had to be up to get ready for school. Junior year at Sky Cove Senior High was tough, but I could do this. Jessie Spencer did *not* let her grades slip. Not even for Sully and Dr. Quinn.

In that hazy place that's not yet sleep but not quite awake, I couldn't help but replay the scene in my mind. And as the dream began to spin behind my eyelids, I allowed myself to be pulled in.

★   ★   ★

The crowd in Thornton's General Store was always large the day of a delivery. It was quite the event in a town as small as Sky Cove, and today was no exception. Even I could not resist wandering up to the second floor to have a look at the new bolts of fabric, despite the fact that I was only here for basics such as flour, sugar, and soap.

Outside, I could hear the beat of horse hooves as more folks arrived at Thornton's to have a look. Dressed in typical 1850s fashion with a long, brown skirt, off-white shirt with long sleeves, and a brown shawl about my shoulders, I looked like any other lady browsing the fabrics. The assembly upstairs grew, and as I was not terribly comfortable in large crowds, I began making my way toward the stairs that led downstairs to the main room of the store.

As I neared the edge of the room, Mr. Herman Smith and his wife Myrtie, who were known for being rather cantankerous, began arguing. She, apparently, was fond of a fabric he thought frivolous and too expensive. Not one to be dissuaded, Myrtie insisted, picking up the bolt of fabric herself. Herman grabbed it away from her, taking her roughly by the arm and swinging the both of them toward the stairway.

And unfortunately, directly into me.

The force of Myrtie, propelled by Herman's strength, knocked me off my balance and I started down the stairway not of my own volition. It seemed to happen in slow motion, the first few steps looking like a clumsy attempt at hopping down the stairs. But midway down, my feet flew out from under me and I tumbled and turned, heading for a landing that would put me directly on my back.

But just before the impact, I crashed into a solid body, not made of wood, but of flesh and bone. The collision didn't seem to affect him. He simply put his arms around me, effectively stopping my fall and keeping me from a very unladylike sprawl on the floor of the General Store.

Looking up, intending to thank my rescuer, I was struck speechless by the deep green eyes of Will Harlow, who I'd long admired from a distance.

In his usual brown trousers and white shirt, he was as easy rescuing me from a fall as he was splitting logs at the mill or throwing heavy sacks of grain over his shoulder. He never seemed to take much of anything seriously, which only added to his allure.

"Might want to be more careful there, Miss Spencer," he said, a sly grin crossing his face. "I can't be around to catch you every time."

My cell phone alarm sounded, and I opened my eyes. Blinking and looking around, I assured myself I was in my room and not in some pre-twentieth century general store.

Sheesh, what a dream. I had to stop watching sappy TV re-runs before sleeping.

Because no way was present-day Will Harlow, high school athlete and popular guy, going to look at science-nerd Jessie Spencer as anything other than a friendly acquaintance.

Normally I used the front door of the school at the end of the day, but an unexpected trip to my locker to retrieve my forgotten calculator made it easier to use the door near the back of the building. As I worked the combination lock, I mentally checked off each class, making sure I had what I needed for homework and studying.

I was nothing if not conscientious.

I'd fought distraction all day long, forcing myself *not* to think about that stupid dream. Thankfully, I'd managed to stay awake despite my lack of sleep, but I figured once I got home, a nap would be the first thing on the agenda.

Grabbing my calculator and closing the locker door, I allowed myself one second to swoon over that moment in my dream where Will's arms had locked around me and I'd looked up into his green eyes. I'd had a major crush on Will for a long time. A crush which was only made worse by my new friend Layla's relationship with Will's best friend Lucas.

Now I was around Will pretty regularly, since Layla and our group of girls hung around with Lucas and Will and the rest of the cross-country guys.

Will was super-nice, but I knew he didn't notice me. At least not in the way a boy notices a girl.

All of a sudden, a group of guys ran down the hall toward the back door. I could hear the commotion from outside when they pushed the door open. Hitching my backpack up on my shoulder, I headed that direction to see what the fuss was about. After all, I had to leave the building anyway.

A fight in the school parking lot had apparently inspired the stampede that now flooded down the hallway behind me. Looked like school jock Todd Miller was pounding on one of the other popular dudes. Over what, was anybody's guess. The cause of the fight didn't really matter. Kids just wanted to see it, and most of the crazy people in the herd didn't seem to care that I was in front of them. They pushed and shoved me like a ping-pong ball in their effort to get outside and witness the brawl.

I'd finally managed to get my footing when one last group of guys barreled toward the door. One of them hit me full force and as the doors to the outside pushed open under their assault, I tumbled out, the freezing January air smacking me in the face.

There were only four steps between the door and the pavement, but in the split second that I sailed downward, I imagined the scene that would result. Me, flat on the blacktop, while the large crowd of onlookers turned their attention from the fight to the awkward nerd who'd fallen down the steps.

I closed my eyes, mentally preparing for the mortification that was imminent.

Just when I expected to hit the ground, I landed against a solid body, not at all made of asphalt. Instead, a pair of arms locked around me, efficiently keeping me from face planting in front of the crowd of people.

I had a momentary flashback to the dream that had plagued the back of my consciousness all day as I looked up to discover my rescuer.

I didn't know whether to be surprised or horrified to find myself staring into the bright green eyes of Will Harlow.

"You okay, Jessie?" The softness of Will's voice always surprised me. At six feet, four inches, he was taller than most guys, with a runner's body that was lean and fit. You'd expect him to have a big, loud voice, but instead he spoke with a quiet, confident tone that left no doubt that a soft voice did not mean wimp or pushover.

Holy cow he was cute. I mean, Not that I hadn't already noticed, but up close he was way better. His jet-black hair was cut short, with just enough left on top to look rustled. And when he smiled his eyes danced.

The fact that he was smiling at me as he helped me back on my feet was confounding. Good grief, I hoped he wasn't laughing at me. Falling in front of a crowd of people, even when pushed by another student, was possibly the most humiliating thing that could happen.

"I'm good," I said, finally finding my voice. "Thanks."

He nodded, still grinning and not taking his eyes off my face. While it was cool to have his attention, the stare was becoming uncomfortable.

"What?" I asked, and he chuckled.

He reached up and swiped at my cheek with his thumb. The gesture shocked me, both with its gentleness and with the jolt of electricity that shot through me, and I almost didn't have enough brain capacity to wonder why he'd touched me.

"You've got a black smudge on your face."

The chilly January wind blustered around, blowing my brown hair into my face. Will raised his hand again, his palm soft against my jaw as he worked once again to remove the smudge from my cheek. Meanwhile, I was stunned into silence.

"Looks like black ink," Will said.

I found my voice. "Probably from my pen." Well, duh.

"I got most of it," he said after a few more swipes.

Not just cute, but nice. Really nice. Could my crush on him get any bigger?

"Thanks," I said, stepping back and putting some distance between the two of us. Before I did something stupid like drool all over him. "And thanks for catching me."

He winked, playful and charming, and said, "No problem."

My heart went *thud*.

Will headed to his car, and as I stumbled my way toward my own, I barely noticed the freezing winter air.

Connect with Amy on Substance B

Substance B is a new platform for independent authors to directly connect with their readers. Please visit Amy's Substance B page (substance-b.com/AmyDurham.html) where you can:

- Sign up for Amy's newsletter
- Send a message to Amy
- See all platforms where Amy's books are sold
- Request autographed eBooks from Amy

Visit Substance B today to learn more about your favorite independent authors.